# NERON

EPISODE ONE

# RISING

# KEARY TAYLOR

First Edition: November 2018
Book design by Inkstain Design Studio
Cover art by Eddy Shinjuku

Taylor, Keary, 1987-
Neron Rising (Neron Rising Saga) : an episode / by Keary Taylor. – 1$^{st}$ ed.

# ALSO BY
# KEARY TAYLOR

*Blood Descendants Universe*

*The Fall Of Angels Trilogy*

*Three Heart Echo*

*The Eden Trilogy*

*The Mccain Saga*

*What I Didn't Say*

# NERON RISING

# ONE

Illegal transactions should never occur this early in the morning.

I shove my feet into my boots, not bothering to lace them up, because that requires brainpower, and I don't have enough of that when the sun hasn't even begun to think about touching the tips of the elite towers. But I do have to think about walking quietly. Dad is still sleeping, and considering what I'm heading to do, I need him to stay that way.

The thick smog hits my lungs as soon as I step out of our tiny cube of a home. It's one of thousands in the Stacks, the low-income corner of this city we call home. I cough, my lungs trying to adjust to all the pollution in the air, and I set down the weaving walkway that zigzags down past the same neighbors I've had for my entire life, before connecting to the skywalk that aims me toward the south end of town.

My connect-link beeps and I hold up my wrist, illuminating a screen against my forearm. A message from "The Mole" displays. *You're late.*

I speak to my wrist and the words appear on the screen. *That's what you get for scheduling this so early.*

Her response displays as an expletive and a searing strike of electricity in my wrist.

Despite the pain, I smirk and shake my head.

"Hey, watch where you're going, knobhead!"

Someone yells the words at me as I bump shoulders with another individual on the skywalk. I turn, making eye contact, glaring and daring them to cause even more of a scene.

"Share the walkway, you cack!" I yell back.

I turn and blend back into the crowd of people walking to and from work.

There are so many bodies I can hardly breathe without taking in the scent of an unwashed worker, or the potent perfume of the next space hog. I'm jostled and bumped into, and no one, except for the cack back there, seems to notice or mind.

It's just a part of life here on Korpillion.

When you're just one of twenty-eight point one billion people, you learn to share the road.

I aim for the alley coming up, but I don't even cast my eyes toward it. I shift to that side of the skywalk and raise my left hand a little.

Just as I pass it, another hand reaches out from the alley, and hooks the straps of a bag over my fingers. A quick and seamless handoff.

It's the reason I pay Crag. I give him the credits he needs to buy his drugs and swill, he hides certain packages around the underbelly of the city until I am ready for them—no one knows the dark and hidden places of Korpillion better than him.

Being a homeless addict on this planet will eat you alive, body and soul, but he gets the job done.

I slip a few blocks further down the skywalk and then duck down a side street, dropping down five flights of stairs until my feet touch the concrete ground of terra level. I slip past dingy, solid steel buildings, tucking around corners.

It smells like metal and rust down this low. The air tastes damp, even though there probably hasn't been a drop of natural rain to hit this ground in over a hundred solars.

It's quieter down here. No one wants to come down this far, so far away from the sun. It's all metal frames, the roots of the towering buildings that are constantly being built taller and taller. Our planet is in a constant race to reach new heights and find the sun through the smog.

So I really don't worry too much as I carry my bag through the silent streets and finally round into a wide opening beneath one of the city's oldest buildings.

Once upon a time, they would have parked transport vehicles here. But that was before they outlawed those on account of their pollution factor and deemed the common man had to walk everywhere.

Our entire lives are now lived within five square kilometers, or however far our legs can carry us.

Now this space is used to store old pipes and broken welding tools.

From the soot that covers everything, I don't think anyone beside our little operation has stepped foot in here in at least fifty solars.

"Told you she'd be at least fifteen minutes late."

I see the man standing beside her reach over and bump his wrist to hers, and hear a small ting, signaling he just transferred her some credits.

She bet the man I'd be late.

"Haven't you heard?" I ask, stepping inside and weaving my way through the abandoned equipment. "It's been scientifically proven that those who sleep in longer are actually smarter than those who are early risers."

I smirk at Reena as I set the bag on an oversized length of pipe that comes up to my waist in height.

Her lips are set thin and she just glares at me, clearly not amused.

But I smile and turn to the bag, unzipping it.

The man beside Reena steps forward, and his eyes fill with the manic gleam of excitement.

"It's exactly as you asked, fit to the measurements you gave me, and it's ready for use," I say, slipping into work mode. I reach inside the bag and pull the gun from it.

The man reaches forward, gently taking the weapon from me, looking it over with what I swear is reverence. Which is actually a relief to me. He doesn't have that malevolent look in his eye like some of the others do. I can only hope he ordered it as a defensive weapon, and not an offensive one.

"With the budget you presented me with, you get two shards of Neron," Reena explains. "Given average use of zero shots fired per lunar, it will last you a lifetime." She looks the man over as she places two, three-inch long shards of glowing blue crystal in his palm. "But if you find yourself in a desperate situation of need, you will get continuous shots for two weeks."

It sends a wave of cold goosebumps across my arms thinking about it. Most weapons have set amounts of shots they can fire. A dozen. A few hundred if they're automatic and you're feeling strong enough to lug around that kind of firepower.

But Neron is pure, clean energy. It packs a lot of punch despite its tiny package.

"You have no idea-" the man begins to say.

But Reena and I both hold our hands up at the same time, stopping him.

"We don't want to know anything about what you're going to do with the weapon, or the Neron," I speak up.

"Less liability," Reena says.

The man nods his head, understanding, because all twenty-eight point one billion people on this planet know that what Reena and I are doing is so illegal, it would get us sent to Crion—the prison planet—for the rest of our mortal days.

"Is everything to your expectations?" Reena asks, folding her hands in front of her.

For a criminal, she sure is elegant, with her poised nose, perfect posture, and smooth, porcelain skin. Somehow her clothes are always perfectly clean, nearly as shiny as her auburn hair.

"It is," the man says. His tone is still breathy, in disbelief, and he can hardly take his eyes off the weapon and the blue Neron crystals in his hand.

"Get us paid so we can all get out of here," I say the words. I didn't really think about them, they just kind of slipped out. They gain me a look of annoyance from Reena.

"Of course," the man says, snapping out of his trance. He extends his wrist to Reena's first, transferring the credits. And then mine.

I look at the screen, and it shows the forty-nine thousand credits transfer to my account. It comes up as payment for sex.

Prostitution isn't looked upon in much of an acceptable manner, but it isn't illegal. If my account were to ever be reviewed, I have to have some kind of explanation as to why I have such large deposits periodically. I have to have a cover story.

"It's been a pleasure working with you, Mr. X," Reena says, packing up her own bag and slinging it over her shoulder.

She calls every client of ours Mr. or Ms. X. We never ask for real names, we'd never want to know.

Turning with her, we leave the man to marvel over his very expensive new toy. We both turn to the right, cutting down the side of the massive base building.

I pause for a moment, fishing a rag out of my bag. Looking at myself in the reflection of the window, I set to washing the band off my face.

There are cameras all over this planet. I'm dealing in illegal transactions on a near-weekly basis. I don't need the cameras knowing my face. So this morning, before I headed out the door, I dipped my fingers in my charcoal-grease mix, and spread it from one edge of my hair, across the bridge of my nose, under my eyes, to the other edge of my hair, masking my face.

I've told Reena she should do the same.

But she never listens to me.

"How many more orders do you expect to fulfill this lunar?" Reena asks as we start walking again. She doesn't look over at me. She keeps her eyes fixed straight forward, almost as if I'm not really here.

Typical. For a criminal, you'd think she was one of the elite space hogs.

"I have two more lined up for delivery before the end of the lunar," I say, looking around to be sure there are no ears within hearing distance. "I have another potential client who hasn't made a deposit yet."

"Keep in touch," she says as we rise up, taking the five flights of stairs before popping back out on the lower skywalk level. Without another word, she hooks to the right, immediately disappearing into the crowd.

I'm not really sure why Reena dislikes me so much. We've been working in correlation with each other for almost four lunars now, and the entire time she's been nothing but chilly and…almost suspicious of me. Maybe it's because she was born into this life of illegal activity and I didn't jump in until I was twenty-two solars. But she's remained frosty this entire time.

I grab something to eat from one of the hundreds of street vendors. The food is bland and tastes fake, because it is. Considering the entire planet of Korpillion is populated from shore to shore, there is no room to farm real food. Every bit of our food comes from off-planet, or is engineered in a lab.

But it keeps us alive. If it can keep so many others alive, I'll survive.

Not that I've ever known any different.

Checking the time, I pick up my pace, bumping into others as I dart down the skywalk. The trams zoom by, rocking everything around them. Ships drift through the sky up above. The planet is awake, and everyone is in a hurry to make it to work.

I aim for the massive building looming up ahead.

I slip into the crowd filing into the building and wait my turn to scan my handprint to clock in.

"Cutting it a little close today," a voice from behind me says.

I scan my hand, looking over my shoulder and glaring at Zayne. "Mind your own business."

"Hard to do when I know how much you need this job," he says, scanning his hand next. When it beeps, he steps beside me, and we head for the narrow door that funnels everyone into the mass of the building, ready for another day at Horne Energy.

"I keep reminding you, it's not your job to worry about me and my dad's financials." I let out an exasperated sigh as we aim for the employee locker room. Unfortunately, our lockers are located right next to each other. "Hasn't been in three lunars."

"Come on, Nova," he says, scanning his hand once more on the door of his locker, opening it. "Just because it's over doesn't mean I can just shut off a solar and a half of history."

I open my own locker and pull out the fresh jumpsuit some staff member put in there last night. I peel off my tunic and unzip my top and bottoms, stripping down to my underthings.

I thought we were past this. But Zayne still gives me a side look as I change and he slips into his own uniform.

Yeah, he's nice to look at. He keeps himself in great shape. His dark hair is on trend, and his jawline could practically cut steel. But he's not mine to stare at anymore, and I was the one to decide that.

"I won't be late tomorrow," I say, turning my back to him as I zip up the front of my black jumpsuit. I grab my fingerless gloves from the locker, and set off across the space toward the doors.

There is a front to this building. There's a grand lobby and big fancy offices. But us grunts don't ever walk through those doors. We come in through the side, and our access dives right into the heart of the building.

I set through the tunnel that immediately branches off the main outlets. I take a lift down and down, and finally it opens, revealing a cavernous opening.

Everyone in the building calls it the Pit of Hell.

There isn't a shred of natural light down here. It smells like steam and grease and metal.

It's the smell of heaven to me.

Pipes and wires and moving components rise and twist in every direction. It's loud and sounds like chaos.

It sounds like a miracle to me.

I head down the walkway, the one that leads directly to my office and workshop.

It's immediately quiet when I close the door behind me. I sit down at my desk, and the screens instantly come to life. My eyes scan the reports and analytics, telling me all the problems I have to fix today.

I work for the largest power plant on the planet Korpillion. We're located in the center of the planet and we send power to this entire side of the globe. Our building spans kilometers of land. It's divided into sections, four different quadrants, with four different teams who take care of what needs to be done.

I'm a member of the third quad. I'm an engineer, that's my official title and what my education was in. I'm also, largely, a mechanic. I keep everything running. I fix problems. I build things to make other things run better.

Others might look at me as a grease monkey, but without me, the planet would quickly lose power.

Zayne Nason, who I've known since I started here three solars ago, works as an information wizard.

That's not what he's really called. But I don't really understand what it is he does, so I dubbed him a wizard.

The report on my holoscreen says there's a problem with the pipes on sub-level 4, so I grab the tools I'll need, and head out.

There's steam leaking from one of the pipes and it's hot as the Underworld here in this cramped corner. Gritting my teeth, I set to the task.

"You there?"

I startle at the voice and smack my head against one of the other pipes above me.

It cracks, and steam starts spilling out of it, too.

I swear, rubbing the back of my head, probably smearing grease into my dirty blonde hair.

"Sometimes you come calling at the very worst times," I say, grabbing a roll of tape and patching the crack temporarily until I can get the parts to fix this new problem.

"I'm sorry," he says. "Are you with someone?"

I roll my eyes and shake my head, even though he can't see me. "I didn't mean that. I only meant that when a voice suddenly speaks inside your head, it has a tendency to startle you and make you crack your head on the pipes you're working on."

"Oh, sorry," his voice comes through, in my brain, like he's a tiny figure standing right inside my skull, speaking directly into my auditory nerve. "Are you alright?"

"I'm fine," I grit my teeth as I use a wrench to pry the slip sleeve loose. "Just a new bump on the back of my head. How is your day?"

He pauses a moment, and I wonder what he's doing. "It's not really day here. I'm on the dark side of a moon."

"Anywhere I might have heard of?" I ask as it finally loosens and I unscrew the part.

I actually hear him chuckle. "Probably not."

"Doing anything interesting there?" I ask. I'm normally better conversation than this, but I'm distracted. I've got to get these pipes fixed or we'll start to lose pressure within a few hours.

"Just work," he responds.

A hissing sound whips my head around, and I see steam spraying out from around my tape. It's too much. If I don't get it under control, the whole pipe will blow out.

"Sorry, I have to take care of this," I hiss, ripping through my bag, praying I've got the right stuff to patch the leak; something better than tape. "I'll connect later, 'K?"

"Alright," he says. "Good luck."

And just like that, I feel him leave my head.

I swear under my breath as I dash for the shut-off valve.

They're going to be mad at me later for doing this, but at least it won't cause a meltdown. I should have done this sixty seconds ago, but it's easy to get distracted when a voice suddenly speaks directly into your mind.

You're supposed to be alone in your head. Sure, your own voice might talk to you, might criticize you, or give you motivation.

But one day, about two lunars ago, there was suddenly this *other* voice.

Clear as day, I felt it there. Like a physical presence. Like somehow this little shard of ice suddenly appeared in the middle of my brain.

"Hello?" a voice called out from it.

I'd screamed in my bedroom as I'd been getting ready for bed. Thankfully Dad wasn't home.

"Are you alright?" the voice called in my brain. "Where are you?"

"Who are you?" I demanded, searching my room for the intruder.

But I knew. I could feel it. Him. He wasn't in my room, or our cube. He was *inside* my head.

"What are you doing here?" he'd asked. "How did you get inside my head? Who sent you?"

"Sent?" I demanded. "How did you… What is happening?"

It went on like this for a good hour. Demanding to know whom the other was. What we were doing in each other's heads.

Somehow, I shut him out.

He was gone.

Only to be there again a few days later. Only he was clearer. Like I could hear him better.

And then, one morning I was getting ready for work, and I suddenly felt like I was somewhere else. Somewhere semi-familiar, but foreign. *I was in *his* head.*

He never would tell me his name. So I had never told him mine. I didn't know where he lived or where he was from. I had no idea what he looked like, but his voice was as familiar as my own.

When the anxiety of having someone randomly pop into my head subsided, I found…a friend. Someone to talk to. And he, likewise.

It became a bi-weekly tradition, to check in with one another, and just…talk.

But now wasn't the time, when I had all this steam burning my face and hands and arms. He'd understand if I connected later.

It takes me an hour and a half, but I finally get the pipes fixed. An idea strikes, a way to potentially make some new pipes. Stronger ones, ones that would never break, never warp, and never leak.

I finally get back on my feet and I slip my audobuds in my ears, and tap the circle on my connect-link that says *The Black Hole of Truth.*

"Welcome back to this highly illegal episode of *The Black Hole of Truth* with Arden Black," a confident female voice comes through, straight to my ears. "Today, I want to talk about something that became my obsession back in my school days. You know, five solars ago, when I still lived on Falbos."

I smile, because she's so bold and brilliant. This is the most listened to spacecast in the galaxy, and the most *illegal* because of her content. Arden Black is constantly dropping hints about where she is and who she is; constantly teasing the authorities, daring them to find her and shut her down.

"I want to talk about the history of the Nero."

I head back toward my office to do some research. But even though I've walked past it a thousand times before, I still stop and stare.

I press pause on the spacecast.

There is a core in each of the quadrants. A massive pillar that runs seven-terra levels below ground, up to the top of the building. Glass keeps it contained and amplifies the glowing blue beauty of the Neron core.

Neron is everywhere. It's energy. It's life. It's in the air we breathe, it's in my blood, it's in every tool I use. It's in all of the food we eat.

It's also found in solid form on certain planets around the Eon Galaxy. In solid form, it can power anything. Weapons. Ships. Buildings. Entire planets. The company I work for, Horne Energy, buys solid Neron and powers every city on Korpillion.

Our modern space travel exists only because of Neron energy.

I might be mixed in the dealings of Neron, but for most, just the word strikes a quake of fear in the back of one's throat.

Because where there is Neron, there is Dominion.

The mega company has been around for over four hundred solars. Once upon a time, it was called Dominion Blue, because Neron is blue in its natural form. But now they've dropped the façade of being just an energy mining company.

They still mine Neron. But it's gone so far beyond that.

Dominion scouts the galaxy for planets rich in Neron deposits. Once they find one, they settle on the planet and establish a mine. They also buy up as much real estate on that planet as they can. They say they employ the locals, but it's little more than servitude. They take over the economy. And then it isn't long until the governments have less power than Dominion.

They take over planets. Once Neron is discovered on yours, almost everyone will move somewhere else in the galaxy. Because no one wants to be subjected to the control of Dominion.

They don't care about families. They don't care about homes. They don't care about destroying landscapes.

They just want the Neron. Neron makes them money. The entire galaxy is dependent on it.

Dominion is the reason Korpillion is so over-populated. Because every other inhabitable planet in all the nearby solar systems have Neron on them. All those residents immigrated here. To a planet that supposedly has no Neron.

Only it does.

Thirty-seven solars ago, Reena McDyer's father discovered Neron while working as a sewer excavator. Knowing what the discovery of the Neron would do to the planet and all of its residents, he kept his discovery from his employer and immediately quit his job. He was a poor man who was struggling to make his way in the world. I doubt he really set out to get into a life of crime, but when you're desperate, you'll do just about anything.

He began dealing Neron.

Neron can be used to power just about anything. A few shards of it can power your home for over a solar with no bills from the power company. It can serve as the firepower for weapons, like the ones I make.

But it can also do other…things.

Like make you see things, things like your short-term potential future. Things like what your most loved one is really feeling. It can make you sharper, quicker. It can heal you. It can even make you age slower.

But only in small doses. Tapping into Neron for personal gain drains it much quicker than using it for energy. The effects of simply holding it are short lived.

Unless you eat it.

Like the Kinduri.

To everyone but Dominion, who hold the majority of the Kinduri in their power, *they* are the real fear. If you see one, with their black lips, black, bleeding eyes, and skeletal forms, you turn and walk the other way.

Because they can do things. They can make you say things. They can read your mind. It's said they can drain your soul.

I've never believed in magic, but I do know for a fact the Kinduri are cursed by the universe for so selfishly consuming what is not theirs.

They're terrifying and strong, and utterly effective.

The only thing stronger than a Kinduri is a Nero.

"Where have all the Nero gone?" Arden's voice speaks in my ear as once more I press play. "I've heard there used to be hundreds of Nero in the galaxy. Maybe even thousands. Because there was once a war between them. A battle between the good and the bad Nero."

But almost all of them have disappeared. There has only been one born in the past eighty-seven solars.

And he, too, is controlled by Dominion.

Even the strongest, most fascinating and powerful being in the universe is controlled by an evil corporation.

I look away from the Neron core as I aim for my office.

I hate thinking about the Nero. It makes me sick. It makes me sad and angry.

Because I think the galaxy would be a very different place if they rose again.

The Nero can do everything that any person in possession of Neron can do, but a hundred fold. Nero are born with a connection to Neron. They don't have to have solid Neron to have a weapon, they can pull it from the air and *make* a weapon of electric Neron. They can read your true emotions. It's said they can read your thoughts if they are strong enough. They can move things simply by manipulating the Neron in everything. Because there is energy and life in everything. I've even heard they can see the future.

The Nero are the real wizards.

"Dominion has nearly driven the Nero extinct," Arden says boldly. "As they've taken over every Neron-rich planet, fewer and fewer Nero were born. The Nero were almost always born on planets with natural Neron, but how many of those exist anymore that Dominion doesn't control?" She pauses for a bit, and the trillions of listeners she has around the galaxy already know the answer. "None."

Dominion owns them all. Except Korpillion, simply because they don't know the Neron is here.

"What happened to Evander Nero?" Arden asks her listeners. "If there ever was a good man, it was him. The second to last Nero known to be born, he fought Dominion every day of his life. He rallied them all, and led the attack on Isroth. He may not have been successful. Cyrillius might have crushed them with his army, with the Kinduri…" she pauses, and I shake my head with her, "but we know Evander Nero escaped Isroth. We know, because he lived to give the prophecy."

Goosebumps flash across my skin.

There isn't a soul alive in the Eon Galaxy that doesn't know the prophecy given by Evander Nero, who saw not only his own future, but that of the entire galaxy.

"Evander Nero promised that another Nero would come," she says. Her voice is soft, a little broken sounding, but hopeful. "Another Nero, who would be strong enough to bring the galaxy back from destruction. Another Nero who could free Neron. And we all know what that means. If Neron is to be free, it would mean the end of Dominion."

A cold shiver works its way down my spine.

Another Nero was found, after Evander Nero disappeared. The last Nero in the entire galaxy.

He could have been a savior. The only person in the galaxy powerful enough to stand up to Dominion.

Instead, they turned him to their side, and made him their puppet.

They turned him into a very, very bad man.

"Where is this savior you promised, Evander?" Arden asks. "Because it certainly isn't Valen Nero."

I feel sick. I feel a million pounds heavy.

So, I pull my audobuds out of my ears and slip them into my pocket.

I shove thoughts of magic and hope out of my head, and turn to my screens, determined to finish this research on something as boring and basic as stronger pipes.

# TWO

"Long day?"

My eyes slide over to the tiny kitchen area as I walk through the door with a grumble. My father is there, preparing our simple dinner.

I sigh, stepping inside and flopping down on a chair, one of two, because that's all we can fit in this tiny space. "Today was one of those days when *everything* decides to break."

"One of these days, there's going to be too many people, and this whole planet is just going to break right in half," he says as he stirs something in a pan.

I huff a laugh, because it honestly feels like the truth. "How was your day?"

He shrugs. "Nothing special. Just work, as usual."

My father, Torin Ainsley, works maintenance at the local school. Day in and day out, he fixes broken sinks, backed-up toilets, scrubs ink off walls, and keeps the power in the building running so the lights stay on for those children.

It's a thankless job. It isn't glamorous. But it has paid our bills my entire life, and it's been stable.

It's where I first found my love for mechanics and engineering, crawling through the underbelly of the school building, fixing the wiring or repairing the ducting.

He taught me a lot of skills the planet no longer values.

Together we eat at our tiny table, a meal of manufactured protein mush and vegetables that barely have enough nutrients to qualify as food.

Our life is simple. Routine. Basic.

We work.

We eat together.

We sleep.

Repeat.

My father is a simple man, but he is reliable.

I look up at him as I chew. His eyes remain fixed on the cracked tableware.

His eyes are gray where mine are pale blue. His nose is round where mine is narrow. His jaw square, where mine is more heart-shaped.

Our only common feature is our dirty blonde hair, but you wouldn't know it now. His has turned silver over the last five solars.

I wonder, as I always have, if I got all of my features from my mother. If I look like her.

When I was old enough to ask why I didn't have a mother when all my friends did, he told me that she died when I was a baby. That it was a construction accident.

They're common on Korpillion, where they constantly have to build higher and bigger to keep up with the growing population.

I hate that this suffocating planet took her from me before I ever had a chance to know and remember her.

"I was thinking," I say as I push the last bite of tasteless food into my mouth. "I have enough saved up now. We should start planning that trip to the coast."

Dad's eyes rise to meet mine and his brows furrow. "With prices of lodging and food on the coast, you'd have to save up for a solar to be able to afford it. Places like the coast aren't for people like us."

He doesn't say it cruelly or spitefully. He says it with resolve. Like it's so far out of reach, the thought is instantly out of his mind again.

"That's the thing," I say, leaning forward and crossing my arms on the table. "I have been saving up for a long while. We have all our bills paid up. We have no debt now. I think we can afford to experience a little comfort and fun."

He gives me a little smile. "That sounds nice, Nova. I'll think about it." But I see it in his eyes, and I know him well enough that I know he really won't think about it.

We work. We eat together. We sleep. We start it all over again.

I give him a little smile that I know doesn't reach my eyes. But I can't find it in me to fight him, to argue and beg. So I pat his hand, and stand to clear and wash the dishes.

With the routine of the day complete and the world growing dark outside, I take the three steps to my bedroom and close the door.

Plain white walls, small bed, even smaller desk. A wardrobe holds the eight different sets of clothes I own. An extra pair of shoes is in the bottom of it.

There is no room for excess on Korpillion.

There is no room for extra children—one per family is regulation. Children are to live with their parents until they marry. There aren't enough housing units on the planet to bend the rules.

I flip the lights off and lay back on my bed, letting my eyes slide closed.

I can feel the connection. Like a little wormhole that goes directly from my brain to his. It's as easy to open as it is to close my eyes.

"Do you ever feel like your life is just going to suck you into an abyss and you're going to simply cease to exist, because it's all the same, over and over, every single day?"

I send the words down in a rush, like liquid spilling down a slide.

"Bad day?" his voice comes through, clear as day.

I let out a breath, and somehow, I know he can hear it. "No." I flop one arm over my eyes. "That's the thing, it was exactly like every other day."

He's quiet for a moment. And for yet another time, I try to picture him. Is his hair dark or light? Is he tall or short? How old is he? What color are his eyes?

"There's something to be said about the comfort of routine," he responds. "We only miss it when it's gone and life is suddenly chaos."

"Sure," I say, because I know the moments of panic that break things up. Like when I got a call four lunars ago that my father had broken his arm and needed emergency surgery. I'd rushed from work and met him at the infirmary. My heart had been in my throat the whole time. I didn't like the feeling of panic.

"But I can't say I particularly feel alive these days." I say the words, and hearing them spoken in my own head, it's like a rounding chorus, repeating the words and the feeling, over and over and over again.

"But you won't leave your planet because of your father." He states the reason I've given him in the past.

My stomach twists. "I just feel stuck."

"If only we could mesh our two lives," he says. "I could use a little more normalcy. Some boring downtime. And you could use some of this chaos and impulse."

"What part of the galaxy are you in now?" I ask. I don't expect an answer, because we never talk details-names, places.

"Just outside a gas planet in the S3 system."

He shocks me when he answers with a simple, direct answer.

"You're not that far away," I say, and to my surprise, a little smile pulls on my lips. "I'm in the U9 system."

I hear him give a little amused sound, and it widens my smile. "Still light years apart, and yet you consider this 'not that far away.'"

Now I chuckle. "It's just the modern galaxy we live in."

It's true. Inter-solar travel has never been faster. If I had the credits, I could get on a ship and be to the S3 system in seven days.

"All this science does come with its miracles," he muses.

We're both quiet for a moment. I roll onto my side, my back facing the door and my boring, mundane reality.

"Have you ever thought about it?" I ask. "We've been connected in this insane, impossible, crazy intimate way for lunars now, but if we ever saw each other on the street, we wouldn't even recognize each other."

He's quiet for a beat, and for a second I'm worried I've said something too personal, too intimate.

"I don't think you'd like me in real life," he says, though it's quiet, regretful.

"Why?" I ask.

But he doesn't respond with words. I just get this…impression. This darker, self-depreciating taste on my tongue.

"You act like I don't know you," I say, hugging my pillow into my chest. "Like I haven't learned anything about you in these lunars we've been connected."

"You hear my voice," he says. "But you're missing so much else. There's a lot more to a person than what they say."

"So you're saying you're hiding a lot of secrets?"

"We all have parts of ourselves that we don't share," he answers cryptically.

I make a thoughtful sound. I don't like the idea, that I don't actually know this person who has direct access to my head very well. That our lunars of conversations haven't given me a very good picture of what he is truly like.

"Doesn't seem fair," I say. "I think you know me pretty well. Maybe that just means I'm really boring."

"I highly doubt that."

I finally smile again. "I need to get some sleep," I say, changing the subject. "I have another boring, routine day early in the morning."

"And you're not a morning person," he teases, proving that I'm right, that he does know me.

I laugh and shake my head, even though he can't see it. "Nope."

"Sweet dreams."

"Good night," I say, and I let him close the connection. Because once he does, I feel so alone in this tiny house, on a planet with twenty-eight point one billion people on it.

# THREE

As hard as I tried, my illegal activity dragged in someone besides me. In the end, it's a big part of what broke us up, but even Zayne on his high horse of worry couldn't resist the allure of a Neron weapon.

I lunge forward, striking my glowing Neron staff to Zayne's long rapier. They connect, sending sparks flying into the dim light. The energy arcs and licks the air, sending out the scent of charged oxygen.

Zayne parries, spinning in a circle, swiping low. He tries this move so often it isn't even difficult to jump, the energy of the blade that really isn't a blade at all, threatening to melt the soles of my boots.

When I land, I take a step forward, striking with both sides of my double-sided staff. He has to move quick, blocking one shot and then another. I see the sweat break out on his brow and he grits his teeth.

With a smile, I deliver one last power strike, which knocks him back three whole steps. I step back and deactivate my weapon. The Neron arcs disappear, leaving me with only a handle piece with a glowing blue core.

"What?" Zayne protests. "You can't just deactivate in the middle of a fight."

"I won," I say with a smile, though I don't look back at him and rub it in his face. "Did you want me to actually try to kill you?"

"It wasn't over!" he yells, taking two steps across the wide, empty space. "You can't just declare yourself the victor. Besides, what kind of a fair fight is it when you have two Neron ends and I only have one?"

"I made your weapon exactly as *you* asked," I say, sliding my double-staff into my bag and zipping it up. I turn to look at him and cross my arms over my chest. "You should have thought about it before you picked something so simple and archaic."

"Not archaic," he argues, deactivating the arc and looking at the beautiful handle left in his hand. "Classic."

I chuckle and shake my head.

"You don't make anything that could cause any true destruction, do you?" he asks, and the mood instantly turns sober.

My eyes immediately leave his and find anywhere else to look. "No, Zayne. Nothing more than personal weapons."

He doesn't say anything, but I know he nods and keeps looking at the floor. "I just want you to be careful. I heard someone talking at the bar last night. Apparently, there's a rumor that the illegal Neron going around Korpillion isn't coming from off-planet."

At that, my eyes snap up. Zayne is looking at me again, and his eyes are pleading with me. He wants me to quit this. To get out of this dangerous, and highly illegal business.

I know it's not good for me, but if I'm ever going to escape this boring, mundane life of mine, I need credits. A lot of them. Enough for an entirely new start, doing something that doesn't make me feel like I'm dying a little bit every day.

"They know about the mine?" I ask, anxiety clutching the bottom half of my stomach with a vice grip.

"I don't know," he admits with the shake of his head. "But they were all in agreement that if it is coming from Korpillion, it needs to stay quiet. No one wants Dominion getting word."

My stomach feels sick at the thought. At the possibility of the mega company moving in and laying claim to everything. Of all the lives it would disrupt. Most wouldn't be able to afford the move off-planet, but Dominion wouldn't leave them with much of a choice.

"Thanks for the warning," I say. "I'll talk to Reena, tell her she needs to be more careful."

"You too, Nova," he says. He heads for the door, his bag slung over his shoulder. He pats my own shoulder, lingering just a bit too long, before he heads out.

I run my hands through my hair when the door closes, letting out a slow breath.

Rumors are dangerous. There are too many ears on this planet and the message changes just a little with each whisper. Who knows what the speculations will sound like by the time they fill the city?

As I turn around and look back in my bag, at the weapon lying there, with a glowing blue shard embedded into the handle, I ask myself: Do I start this in hopes that I'll someday get caught? Do I do it because I'm bored? Do I do it because I want everything—*everything*—about my life to change?

It's not something I want to admit to myself. I don't relish in being a criminal. It's not like I dreamed about being an arms dealer when I was a little girl.

I found I was good at something. I went into it for profit.

But that doesn't capture the whole of it.

I pull my staff back out and stare at the glowing blue shard of Neron. Before I think too much about it, I unclasp the small latch and roll the shard out onto my palm.

A wave of electricity washes over my entire body at the contact. I feel the power sink inside me, from the top of my head, down to my smallest toenail. I even feel it in my hair.

There are people in the galaxy who get addicted to Neron.

They don't consume it like the Kinduri, but they crave possessing it. Having it on their person. They relish in the feeling it gives them. In the power they can hold for even just a small span of time.

They can't stop.

They spend every credit they have on obtaining the illegal Neron.

They'll waste their entire life away searching for a fix.

I love the way I feel when I hold Neron. I *love* it.

So I don't let myself touch it more than once a solar, at best. Because I know myself, and I know with how much I love this feeling, I would become one of those addicts.

But for now, I let my eyes slide closed. I let the Neron rush through me. With the simple contact of my skin, it's like it bonds with me, becoming one. I'm instantly aware of all the other Neron that surrounds me: in the air, in the walls of this building, far beneath my feet. I feel it in my blood.

Neron is everywhere.

Neron is energy. Neron is life.

I feel good, because the Neron is healing me. Any small bruise, any cracked finger. Any breaks deep inside me, Neron finds them and heals them.

For this moment, when I am holding this Neron, I am ageless. Time has stopped.

Though it's dark with my eyes closed, movement draws my

attention. The air is very still and I realize I'm not breathing.

A shape steps through the shadowy fog. I find broad shoulders. Strong legs. A proud jawline.

I squint in the dark, searching for the face of this person. But it's dark.

He, I realize it is certainly a male figure, reaches out a hand toward me.

At first I think it's to ward me off, or maybe to push me away.

But as I once more look for his shadowed face, I think that maybe he's reaching for me. Inviting me.

A feeling of familiarity tugs inside of me. I slowly extend my hand. I take two steps forward.

But, just before our fingertips can touch, the entire universe collapses in on us, and it all ends with an explosion of blue Neron.

I drop the blue shard and take five steps back with a startled yell. I bump into a wall and leave myself there, breathing hard and panicked.

I've never actually seen anything when holding Neron. I've felt things, felt connected to people's emotions. But I have never, ever seen anything.

I don't know what that was, or who that was. But I don't want this feeling of heaviness and dread looming in my chest ever again.

With the edge of my tunic, I grab the Neron shard, secure it back in the center of my staff, and pack up.

It's one benefit of being mechanically inclined with a mind for engineering. I found this base level of our cube building a few solars ago. The power system it was operating on had to be over a hundred solars old. After talking with the building manager, I told him I could cut his power costs down to ten times less than what he was paying. If he would pay for the equipment, I could build and install it.

In exchange, he gave me use of the left-over space without question and without ever stepping foot inside.

I would take care of any problems with the system should they arise.

Zayne and I use the space to play with our toys.

Here, I pretend I'm something that I'm not. Here, I pretend that my life has more meaning than it does.

# FOUR

"I confirmed the rumors," I growl at Reena as she bustles around the shop. "I spent two hours in that bar and overheard two different groups talking about on-planet Neron. You're not being discreet enough."

"They have no way of proving that the Neron came from Korpillion," she says, hardly missing a beat. There are five other workers here in the processing room. We're a half a kilometer closer to the surface level than the actual mine. Huge, solid crystals of Neron as big as my head line shelves. The workers operate machinery I helped develop to split them into smaller, more discreet and portable-sized crystals, ready for distribution. "All Neron looks the same."

"You need to take this seriously," I say, taking a step forward and grabbing her arm, making her stop and look at me. "If Dominion finds out there's Neron here, I want you to imagine the consequences. Korpillion is the *only* inhabitable planet in the T, U, and V system that isn't owned by Dominion. Do you really want the displacement of all those people on your hands?"

Reena finally meets my eyes. She stares at me, and I realize why she unsettles me so much. She's cold. Her eyes are like ice. I really don't think she cares about anything.

Except me being on time.

"Dominion sweeps the systems once every fifty solars," she says. And all the little hairs on the back of my neck stand straight up. "Did you know that?"

I didn't.

"Their technology constantly changes, it gets better and better every solar," she explains. "Since Dominion was founded, they have swept the entire galaxy approximately eight times. It has been forty-six solars since they last scanned Korpillion."

Which means our planet has only four more solars until Dominion returns and scans Korpillion with far more advanced technology than last time.

"Dominion discovering our Neron has always been inevitable," Reena says in a cool, quiet way. "It doesn't matter if rumors spread to every corner of the planet. This will all be over in four solar's time, anyway."

"Why haven't you told anyone?" I breathe. "They're going to come and our planet will be gutted. If people knew now, they could prepare. They could move off-planet before things get bad."

Reena jerks out of my hold and goes back to her work. "Don't be foolish, Nova. There are twenty-eight point one billion people on this planet. It would take decades to evacuate them all. Not a notable fraction of them could leave before Dominion comes."

"So you're just going to let everyone get screwed over?" I demand. "You and about a dozen others know for a fact that there is Neron on this planet. You are one of the only people who could do anything about this, who could make a difference, and you're not going to do a slam thing?"

She turns on a grinder and the noise of the machine fills the entire space as it pulverizes the Neron into a fine powder. My pulse pounds in my ears as I watch her, being so calm, continuing as though nothing is wrong. Finally, she switches off the machine and scoops the sparkling blue material into a glass vial.

"I plan to make enough money for me and my crew to get as far away from this planet as possible when they come." She caps off the glass vial and sets it on a shelf with a line of others. "We have four solars to prepare." Her eyes rise to meet mine. "I suggest you do the same."

My gut is hollow and full of a million pounds of Neron at the same time. My mouth opens to say something, but I can't find any words. It closes once more.

My connect-link vibrates and I automatically look down at the screen that lights up on my forearm. It's a message from my father that dinner is ready; he wonders where I am.

"Imagine the chaos," Reena says as she moves onto the next task in her shop of crime and magic. "The panic that would happen. The effect on the economy. The entire planet would collapse within weeks. It's not a perfect world. But it's better this way."

And her words make my insides harden. They ignite a fire in the pit of my stomach. I see it in her eyes, her cold, calm eyes. I won't change her mind. My words won't make a difference.

"You're wrong," I say before turning on my heel and stalking out of the cramped space.

We're eight terra-levels below ground, so it's quite a climb up through the twisted service tunnels of the sewer systems to get back to the surface. I feel like I'm suffocating by the time I level out.

I'm drowning. I'm twisted up. I can't breathe. I'm conflicted.

Dad can tell there's something wrong as we eat our dinner. I know all of my emotions are rolling off me in waves, and I hardly touch my food. But it's one of the great things about him—he understands when I'm filled with too much. I let my emotions get the best of me sometimes, and he knows when not to prod so I don't explode.

So he leaves me alone.

"I'm going out," I say that night after I've cleaned the dishes. "You need the rest, so don't wait up for me."

I shrug on a jacket and slip out the door before he can protest or ask me where I'm going.

It's dark outside, but not really. The sun set about thirty minutes ago, so the sky is black when I look up, other than the moon that sits high in the sky. It looks like it's neon blue, but only because it's reflecting back all the artificial light from Korpillion.

There are signs and glowing advertisements everywhere. There are lights turned on in windows, office buildings. In the towering elite buildings, they flash light shows and display different colors illuminating their homes.

It's dark outside, but so slam bright.

I stuff my hands in my pockets and set down the skywalk. I don't think about where I'm going, but my feet carry me there automatically.

There's a service door that looks shut, but isn't locked. It enters the side of one of the tallest buildings in this sector. I slip inside, closing the door behind me, and begin the climb.

I've heard that there are other planets where the residents have obesity problems. Not on Korpillion. When you have to walk anywhere you want to go, when the cities are more vertical than horizontal, you climb a lot of stairs. Our food is engineered to be the perfect balance for survival, and to keep people just healthy enough.

No one is getting fat on this planet; the government makes sure of that.

So I don't struggle when I climb all these stairs.

Fifteen minutes later, I push open another door. It lets out onto a landing. It isn't large. To the left, there is the service equipment to keep the upper half of this building cool. There's a landing just big enough for maybe a chair, and behind it, there's a ladder that rises up to the roof of the building.

I could go to the top, but it isn't as private. There's access up there to the residents who can afford to live in this building. I don't feel like getting caught.

I lean against the railing that prevents me from falling ninety-six floors to my death, looking out over the city.

It all looks the same. Tall building after tall building, all reaching for the sky. It's an endless jungle of concrete and steel. Where there were once roads where people used their personal transport vehicles, the space has been filled with more buildings. We get around using the skywalks that snake their way between the looming towers. Our lives are lived in an endless maze.

It's kind of beautiful, in a way. People created this. This didn't just appear here. They had to imagine it, design it, build it. It's taken centuries.

And the lights, while loud and bright, they're kind of beautiful against the backdrop of the dark sky and dark concrete.

Sometimes I feel bad about how bored I am with life here.

This is supposed to be the good place.

But that's all going to come to an end.

"You there?" I ask down the connection.

It's like I can feel him moving, hear him rustling, and then sliding into a quiet, private room. "I'm here."

I breathe a sigh of relief at the sound of his voice in my head. "I have to warn you, I'm probably not going to be a very pleasant person tonight."

"I'm not a very pleasant person most of the time," he says, and I swear I can hear a little bit of a smile on his face. "What's wrong?"

I look out over the city, and I can see everything that's wrong. All these people. Suddenly I feel responsible for all of them. "Have you ever had a secret?" I ask.

"I don't know a single person who doesn't have secrets," he answers. His voice is so calm. There's this low, deep timbre to it. There's something about it that's unique. I've never heard a voice that sounds like his.

"Well, have you ever had a secret that would affect billions of people?"

My stomach twists in knots just at the thought of it.

"I can't say that I ever have had a secret of that scale," he confesses. "Surely, you don't actually mean billions."

I huff one short laugh and nod my head. "Actually, I do. And the thing that sucks about it is that I could tell people, but it would create so much chaos, I might actually make things worse. I hate that. I hate it so much, because it makes me feel responsible."

"One person can't be held accountable for billions," he says. His words are like a soft touch, like a hand on my back, rubbing for comfort and support.

"Sure they can," I argue, even though I want to accept his words. I'm in a self-depreciating spiral right now, and I have no intent to get myself out of it at the moment. "Look at Cyrillius. He's destroyed trillions of lives. And he doesn't even feel guilty about it."

Just saying his name makes my mouth taste bitter. As the heir and owner of Dominion, he makes all the calls that affect every single solar system. He could make the galaxy a better place. He could stop the centuries of greed and money. But he's only taken things twenty steps further than his father and his grandfather before him.

"Seems like a little bit of a jump, comparing yourself to him," he says quietly. "Just a few days ago you were complaining about your boring life, and now you're hiding a secret that could affect everyone on your planet?"

"Pretty insane how quickly life can change," I muse. Though, really, nothing has changed at all. Other than now I have to figure out how to get me and my dad, and Zayne, off-planet. "Know of anywhere good left in the galaxy?"

"Suddenly you're also ready to move planet?" he asks. There's a thoughtful probe to his tone.

I shrug, even though he can't see it. "Know of any place?"

This is where I hate this part of our connection. I hear his voice. But that's it. I can't read his body language. I get impressions sometimes, but I don't know if those are real, or my brain filling them in.

I want to read his face right now. I want to have something to fill these longer pauses, to decipher what he's thinking.

But I have nothing but his voice, echoing in my brain.

"Do you really think there's any such thing as a good place, anymore?" he finally asks.

I consider his question as I look out at Korpillion.

This is supposed to be a good place. But, as I look at it, I see the race for credits. I see advertisements flashing bright in my face. I see businessmen talking to prostitutes who are only interested in their connect-link accounts. I see jobs, so many of them, that no one takes pride in, they just do it because it allows them to survive.

I think of Reena, whose goal isn't to save anyone but herself and her crew.

I even think of my dad, who has no joy in life. He just puts his head down and survives.

"I don't know, anymore," I say. I hate the confession, but I am honestly not sure.

"I've been to a lot of places, and all I've seen everywhere is the innate drive to survive," he says into my head. "People will do whatever it takes to survive."

"I wonder when we lost everything else," I say. "The few books that were stored before all of that was lost talk about all these other things, these principals. Honor, glory, love. When did we become a galaxy full of survivors?"

He doesn't answer, because really there isn't an answer. These are just the deep thoughts spoken out loud between two strangers connected by a power neither of us understands.

"I wish I was there with you," he surprises me with his honest words.

I straighten a little, and a smile creeps onto my face. "I wish you were here, too." I pause, letting that confession fill me. "Do you think we could ever meet in real life?"

He takes a considering pause. "I think we have to be careful what we wish for, sometimes."

I don't know what that means, and I don't know why he said it when he just said he wished he were here with me.

"Just tell me the first letter of your name," I say. I'm desperate right now. I don't want to be alone. I want something real. I don't just want this air that's surrounding me instead of the person I wish was here.

"No," he immediately says, but I hear a smile in his voice.

"Oh, come on," I egg him. "What harm is there in just telling me a letter?"

He pauses for a beat, and I feel it, he's teasing me. "It's not A and it's not Z."

"Great," I say sarcastically. "That's helpful."

"You're welcome," he says, and I can just imagine a smug smile. "It's only fair you give me yours now."

"You won't tell me yours, but you want me to be straight about mine?" I say in protest.

"You're your own master."

I smile. "It starts with an N."

I hear him groan. "Your name is Nova, isn't it?"

My eyes roll of their own accord and I actually laugh at myself.

"Really, the most common female name in the galaxy?" he eggs.

"It's not like *I* picked it!" I defend. "My dad says he loved that name and so that's what I became. Along with about ten million other girls on this planet."

There's happiness surrounding that little place in my brain where he lives. This is nice. I actually feel alive here. I feel real, even though if I told anyone else what was happening right now, they would think I was crazy.

"I need to go, Nova," he says, putting a little emphasis on my name.

"Alright," I say, disappointed that he's leaving me. "I'm going to figure out your name. Next time we talk, I'll get it."

"Good luck with that," he says.

I smile, but only for a second longer until he says goodbye. Leaving me alone in the middle of this doomed planet.

# FIVE

Alone in my room, I do research.

On my personal holotab, I search the galaxy for a safe planet to move to. There aren't any Neron-free planets in the solar systems near ours, thus the reason Korpillion is so overpopulated. There is one in the X sector, but the second I get the estimate for a ticket on a ship for three of us, I know it's not in the scope of possibility.

It's discouraging. There are only five livable planets in systems close enough to be feasible. One of those is the desert planet, Starvis, and *no one* immigrates there. The locals there are said to be near savages who are suspicious of any outsiders. They're known for violence and endless, primitive war.

The closest planet to us, and the least expensive to move to is almost exactly like Korpillion. It's overpopulated and the vast majority of the population lives in poverty.

I'm not looking for my home planet 2.0.

That leaves two other possibilities. After some research, I decide my goal is Panus. It has a good variety of landscape, the northern sphere is an ice continent, the southern tip is desert tundra, but the center, along the equator are four tropical continents that are livable. It isn't insanely populated because not everyone can deal with the rainfall they receive.

Rain sounds kind of nice. I've never actually seen real rain. It gets sucked out of the sky the moment a cloud appears because we have to regulate all our water so strictly.

But holy slag, the cost. I do the calculations.

With the current number of Neron weapons I'm building and selling every lunar, it's going to take me almost five solars to save enough money.

I want to be off Korpillion and settled on Panus well before Dominion comes looking for the Neron here. I want to be gone a solar before.

I'm going to have to start hustling.

It's time to get to work.

THE VERY FIRST THING I do is get a list of names from Reena. She's face to face with these kinds of people way more than I am. I, at least, have a legal day job. She runs the crime circuit all day, every day. She's dealing Neron to junkies and elite space hogs.

So she knows those who might potentially be interested.

I reach out to the first five people on the list. And I breathe a sigh of relief when one of them gets back to me.

She wants to meet.

So late at night, I change into all black. I pull on my boots. I don my fingerless gloves. And because I can't afford to be tracked on the city's cameras, I take a jar of black smudge, and rub it around my eyes, across the bridge of my nose, stretching from my eyes, back to my hairline.

I leave my hair down, a wild mane of dirty blonde waves.

I want to be a good daughter. Everything my father has done my entire life was so we can have a good, peaceful life. But he's taken care of me all this time. I'm doing this so I can take care of him. Take care of us.

The woman wants a whip. What she wants a whip for, I'm not going to ask. She tells me how long she wants it, how thick and long the handle should be, and she is very specific about how much Neron she wants it to hold.

It's a lot.

I should question what her intentions are. I should maybe consider that this isn't something I should make, because it will hold way too much power.

But I can't afford to have a conscience for the next three solars.

I have to get us off this planet.

So, with her specifications, I go to work the next morning. I stay late. I take the elevator down four floors from my office. I go through the hidden door I installed. I enter my workshop, buried in an old core that was abandoned long before I came to work here.

Piece by piece, I begin building that whip.

I tap the icon on my connect-link that says *The Black Hole of Truth*.

Arden Black's voice comes through my audobuds.

"This is the kind of stuff that makes me sick," she says, and I hear it in her voice. It's heavy. It's weighted. "You know my sources are spread throughout the galaxy. There is no galaxy-wide news and truth without all of you."

She pauses for a long moment, and I feel the darkness she's feeling, and I don't even know what she's going to say yet.

"I had five, yes you heard that right, five sources contact me yesterday, from the planet Hogwa. As you well know, the planet in the T5 sector was taken over eight solars ago. When Dominion found Neron on their planet, they executed their normal routine and dominated the planet, forcing a population of three billion to either move off planet, or work for them."

I shake my head as I pull the metal from the forge, pouring it into the forms.

"Initially, there was a fight, but you know Dominion's numbers. You know their army. They came with their half a million soldiers, and Hogwa's governments didn't stand a chance. It's been eight solars of servitude since then, for the seven hundred thousand people left on that planet."

It makes my stomach sick. Two point three billion people had to leave their home planet and settle somewhere else, because Dominion came and claimed the Neron as theirs.

Power is an ugly thing. Motivation purely for money is evil.

"I had no idea until yesterday that for the past six lunars, Hogwa was planning revenge. They had planned for freedom. I don't know the details, but they were going to war."

I place my hands on the table, my head hanging low as I wait for the metal to cool. I want to hope, that there's a chance that any planet could rebel against Dominion and win.

But not one planet, in the four hundred solars Dominion has been in power, has won against them.

"On the eve of their strike," Arden continues, "*The Dominion* arrived. The Nero came. They knew. And while the population still worked in the mines, while they went about their daily duties, the

Nero stood on the roof of their command center. And in an instant, half the population dropped dead."

I jerk upright, my eyes wide, my stomach clenching.

"My sources say it's like their skulls spontaneously crushed inward," Arden says, her voice breathy, but angry. "Like wadding up a piece of paper in your hand. Their skin glowed Neron blue, just before they died."

I hold a hand over my mouth, trying not to imagine it in detail, but finding it impossible.

Half of the population of an entire planet.

Dead. Instantly. Because of Dominion's Nero.

"You just can't imagine it, the power the Nero have," Arden says. "But all five sources confirm the same thing. One man, one evil puppet, killed 350,000 people yesterday, and he didn't have to lift a finger to do it."

Emotion pulls into my eyes. I squeeze them closed, refusing to let tears fall.

This is the power of Dominion. This is what they do. Out of greed and power lust.

This…this is why I have to get off this planet.

This is why I'll spend every waking moment working.

I think about the credits and my ticket off this planet, and I get back to work.

# SIX

"How many credits do you have saved up?" I ask Zayne.

He looks over at me and his brows furrow together. "Isn't that one of those kinds of questions you aren't supposed to ask?"

I look back down the skywalk, stepping sideways to avoid a woman talking animatedly on her connect-link, pushing myself into Zayne's side. For a second, it's familiar. We used to walk this very same path all the time, our arms tucked around each other, looking at one another like we were the brightest stars to one another.

But, now, I just immediately step away and focus on the path that leads to the bar.

"I just..." I say. I don't know how much to say. I didn't think of a good lie to cover why I need to know how much money he has. If he can contribute to his ticket, it's all the faster we can get off this planet. "I have a feeling I have more saved up than you do, and I want to see if I'm right."

I raise an eyebrow at him.

There. Make it a competition. That sounds normal for me.

He gives me an annoyed side look. "Seriously? You want to make this a competition? You're forgetting one thing, Nova. I don't engage in criminal activity."

Okay. He's caught me there. It really wasn't a fair question. "Fine," I say. "I know exactly how many credits I have saved up if you don't count the income from my…creations."

Zayne looks over at me again, clearly annoyed at my questions. "Not that it's any of your slam business, but I've got about thirty-thousand credits saved up after paying off my debts for school."

I swear under my breath as we step into the bar and head toward our regular table. As soon as we sit, the waitress takes our order— the usual, oxygen-infused calypso and a basket of fried protein.

"Are you seriously going to judge me?" Zayne asks, giving me an annoyed look. "How much do you have, Queen Nova?"

"Ninety-two thousand," I say. "If you exclude the…extra credits."

"Holy slag," he declares, his eyes bugging for a moment. "And with the extra benefits of your alternative lifestyle?"

"Just under four-hundred thousand," I say, keeping my voice

down. "Are you sure you don't have anything else? How much do you think you can set aside by the end of the solar?"

The waitress drops off our drinks and I immediately grab mine, taking a long draw.

"What's going on, Nova?" Zayne asks, folding his arms over the table. He leans in close, because there are dozens of other people crammed in this tiny bar and there are always ears listening to everything. "You look entirely mooned out, like you're going to hurl at any moment. Are you in some kind of trouble?"

I take another long draw from my drink, which was a bad idea, because I really do feel like I'm going to throw up.

Zayne and I might not be together as a couple anymore, but he's still the one and only friend I have. He's my best friend, even if it's by default.

"I talked to Reena a few days ago," I confess. Maybe it's the drink flooding my brain with too much pure, clean oxygen, but my lips open before I give them permission to do so. "I told her about the rumors going around, and she didn't give a slam."

Zayne pulls his drink toward him, but he doesn't raise it to his lips. "And is there a reason why?"

My eyes finally rise up to meet his. "Did you know that Dominion sweeps every solar system once every fifty solars, scanning for Neron deposits?"

His face instantly loses its color.

I don't have to explain any more than that. He knows exactly what it means.

"How much longer until they come through again?" he asks in a low voice.

"Four solars," I say quietly, looking around the bar to be sure we won't be heard. But maybe I should let someone overhear. Maybe I should stand on this table and tell everyone as loud as I can.

*There is Neron on Korpillion. And Dominion is going to come for it in four solars.*

Slag, Reena's right.

If everyone knew, the whole planet would freak out. The economy would instantly collapse, and then no one could afford to get off-planet.

"I've got a plan to get us off Korpillion," I say, leaning in close. My eyes scan the crowd, and suddenly they all feel like competition. Not everyone will get off, but I slam well plan to be long gone. And I hate myself for thinking like Reena. "Me, you, and Dad are getting off this planet and going to Panus. But it's going to take a lot of credits."

I see the understanding dawn in his eyes as to why I was asking about his savings. "How much?"

"Two point four million," I say the number that makes my stomach sick. "Eight hundred thousand each."

Zayne curses and sits back in his seat. His fingers tangle in his hair and he looks at me with this hopeless expression. He shakes his head. "Nova, that would take me ten solars to save enough just for me, and that's if I don't have to spend a single credit between now and then."

"Keep your voice down," I hiss at him, grabbing his wrist and pulling him in back toward me. He looks around, realizing his mistake. "That's why you're going to stop judging me for my alternative employment. That's why you might have to start helping me now and then."

I see it in his eyes that he hates the idea. He hates every syllable of it.

But I've said the name Dominion now.

The game has changed.

"Well, well," an annoying voice croons from just a few feet away. "Look who is sitting together, fighting as usual."

I look over to see Zina walking toward us, a huge glass of calypso in her hand. "To most of the world, it would look like we've gone back in time, but I know this," she says, wagging her finger between Zayne and I, "ended lunars ago. How do you stand it, Nova? Spending time with him like he didn't end things?"

"Stay out of it, Zina," Zayne growls.

"There's nothing else happening on this planet," she says with a drunk smile. "Might as well stir some slag up."

"Try not to fall off the skywalk on your way home," I say through my teeth.

She gives a little laugh and a sigh. "How do you feel about it?" she asks, looking at me with eyes that are beginning to get that glossy, starry look to them.

"About what?" I ask, using every ounce of patience I have.

"About the fact that Zayne *so* wants to get back with you?" she says, her voice suddenly very clear and filled with ill intent. "About how he watches you constantly. About how he reserves every single one of his weekends for you, the girl he let go for reasons unbeknownst to everyone at work."

"It's called private business because it's private," I say. I'm trying really, really hard not to overthink what she's said. I know all those facts. But not everyone knows what they think they know.

It might seem like Zayne broke it off from our fights over the last lunar of our relationship. But it was me who finally called it off.

"It's just kind of pathetic, you know," she says as she leans in, her face just a foot away from both of ours. "You two just keep stringing each other along. Move on. Get one last bang out of your systems if it helps end things."

I didn't mean to. I really didn't.

But it was just suddenly done and over.

I slap her.

Hard.

Across the face.

Her drink spills, slopping over the table and on Zayne's right arm. She stands there frozen for a solid five seconds with her mouth open in a little O, the mark of a red handprint rapidly appearing on her face.

Slag.

"Zina, I-"

But I don't get a chance to actually apologize, even if she really deserved it, because she launches herself at me, hands around my throat, taking the both of us to the ground.

Everyone had to be bored. It's the only explanation, because within thirty seconds, everyone is fighting.

Zayne was trying to pull Zina off me. I was trying to kill Zina. She was yelling for her friends. They were on top of us. And then it was everyone throwing punches at everyone and blood and screaming and swearing.

And then there were three other women on top of me. One had their hands around my throat. One was actually pulling my hair, and ripping some of it out, and the other was kicking me in the ribs.

I'm reckless. It's been the bane of my father's existence. Because under pressure, I tend to explode. I don't think. Things just happen and then I'm left with the consequences that follow.

The bar ignites in brilliant blue, and the arc of my staff is crackling one inch from Zina's face. Her girlfriend instantly backs away, a lock of her hair falling to the floor in a smoking mess as the Neron cuts through it.

The entire bar instantly freezes and every eye turns to me.

Oh, slag.

All three girls scramble away from me and the entire bar steps back as far away from me as they can. Except for Zayne, who is looking at me where I'm still laying on the floor, with horror in his eyes.

Now *my* mouth is frozen in that stupid looking O. I press the power and the Neron arc instantly dies, and I'm just holding a seemingly harmless looking handle.

Neron weapons aren't unheard of on Korpillion, but they are exceptionally rare. Rare enough ninety-eight percent of the population has never seen one. I'm the only one on the planet that I know of that makes them, but that doesn't mean others don't have them illegally imported from other parts of the galaxy.

Showing off a Neron weapon in a public way might have just put a life sentence on my head.

"Come on," Zayne says, extending a hand to me and pulling me to my feet. I keep my head down, letting my hair fall in front of my face. No one was paying attention to me when we entered the bar, I don't need to let them have a few seconds more to memorize my face so they can report it.

We dart out of the building, and instantly slip into the crowd.

"Seriously?" Zayne hisses through his teeth. "Were you really going to kill her, or were you just feeling the need to show off?"

"Of course I wasn't really going to kill her!" I say, my voice frantic. "I don't know what happened. First there was the slap, and then I grabbed the staff. It was all just…fast."

"Well, what are you going to do now, Nova?" he says. He's panicking and I should be panicking, but my brain hasn't quite caught up yet. "Because most of those people in that bar might not be able to identify you, but Zina and her crew sure will. If she turns you in, you're going straight to jail."

She *will* turn me in. No doubt about it. She's wanted Zayne for a solar now and she's tried every tactic she could think of to break us up when we were still together. It's been weekly meltdowns from her when we stayed so close after the break up.

"I…" I stutter. My brain is tripping over itself, trying to come up with a solution. "She doesn't know where I live. As long as I don't go back to our regular spots, it's not like we're likely to see each other ever again."

"Except at work," Zayne points out like I'm an idiot.

My eyes slide over to him. "That was the part I hadn't told you yet."

His look darkens. He knows he's not going to like what comes out of my mouth next.

"I make twenty times more credits making...what I make, than what I earn at work," I say, keeping my tone down. We're just walking down a random skywalk, because if anyone follows us, me, I don't want to lead them straight to my home. I've got to disappear. "With how many hours I'm working right now, I can only get one weapon made a week, at best. If I just quit the day job and work for myself full time..."

He swears again, dragging his fingers through his hair. "This is insane, Nova. You've always been reckless, as we just saw back at the bar. But this takes it to an entire new level. You're...you could end up getting caught. You could go to jail at any point. You'll be working with the lowlifes of the planet. You could get killed!"

"And what other choice do I have, Zayne?" I yell. I round on him, dragging him to the side of the skywalk. The crowd immediately shifts around us, flowing past. "Do you want to be here when Dominion comes? When they take over everything? When they bring their army as guards and their mining crew that forces the locals into endless work?"

The look in his eyes tells me he doesn't. But he's not going to admit it.

"There is no other option," I say, sounding desperate. "You're never going to make enough in time. Dad is never going to make enough in his entire lifetime. But *I* can do this."

My throat feels tight.

I might not love Zayne the way I once did.

But he's family.

I don't have anyone in this world beside him and my dad.

I don't like people. Maybe that makes me a bad person. But, generally I don't. People lie. People are out for their own gain. We all are.

So I keep my circle small. And hold on to those few for dear life.

"Stars, Nova," Zayne finally says. He grabs me and pulls me into his arms, tucking my head under his chin, and holds me tight. "Why do you have to be so slam epic all the time?"

I laugh, even though there are tears pricking in my eyes. I'm overwhelmed. I'm tired. I'm stressed.

But I'm too stubborn to give up.

"What can I do to help?" Zayne finally says. And I feel it. This is him giving in. This is him accepting that we have to do what we have to do.

Because we're a pair of those survivors in this galaxy.

# SEVEN

Catching criminals on Korpillion is nearly impossible. There are just too many people and too many places to hide and lay low.

Zina might have turned me in, I'm sure she did. But will anyone believe her, that the grease monkey at Horne Energy, has a Neron weapon? Finding me will be nearly impossible. Company records are a mess at best. I wish them good luck in tracking me down.

But I immediately quit my job.

The night I exposed myself with my Neron staff, Zayne and I spent all night preparing.

I immediately rented a small warehouse in a low level—a shady deal done in the middle of the night. We went back to Horne Energy, and being very careful not to be seen, we moved all of my equipment out. It took us six trips, with both of us carrying armload after armload.

To my dad, nothing has changed. I still leave at the same time. I come home around the same time.

But I'm working on weapons full time, now. With Zayne's help. He hasn't forgiven me that he had to quit his job, too, in order to protect me, so no one could find him either and ask him questions.

In two weeks, I have five new clients and two more potential ones. I can build a weapon in about three days instead of the week or more it was taking me before.

In two weeks, I make an additional eighty thousand credits.

This is going to work. I'm going to make it happen.

I'm going to get us off this planet.

We're just wrapping things up one evening when I suddenly feel *his* presence.

"Can I talk to you in a little bit?" I think back. Because Zayne is standing just beside me, working on his holotab, where there is a design for a new fire-cannon displayed.

"Of course," he answers back.

"Hey," I say out loud. "I need to get these joints figured out. It could take me a while. Why don't you head home and call it a night?"

He looks up at me, a slight question of *why* in his eyes. But it doesn't linger long. It's been a longer than normal day already. He's tired. He's done.

"You're not meeting with a client tonight, are you?" he asks, giving me a side look.

"Not tonight," I say, my tone condescending and exasperated. "But Crag will be stopping by to hold onto Mr. X's order until he can meet for delivery in four days."

Satisfied that I'm not going out to do a delivery by myself tonight, he nods and shuts off the holotab. "Don't stay all night," he says as he walks toward the huge metal door. "Torin will start worrying in about an hour."

"Stop worrying about me, you old woman!" I call after him. He flips me a vulgar gesture as he walks out.

I smile, shaking my head.

It seemed ridiculously impossible that we could stay friends like this after breaking up when we were together for such a long time. But, somehow, we have.

The truth was, I started getting bored with life in the last few lunars we were together. I could see exactly how the rest of my life was going to play out. Zayne had dropped talk about getting married here and there, and I knew that before too long he would propose and I would eventually marry him, and we would eventually have a child and raise it on this over-crowded planet.

I hated it.

I hated the entire vision and future of it.

Zayne was great. He was stable. I knew he loved me. I knew he would give me a good life.

But I just couldn't stand the thought of nothing really changing. Ever.

So, one night, I stayed late at work. I made this incredibly simple thing: a double-ended handle.

And I stole a small shard of Neron from work.

It took me two weeks to fine-tune it to work. But eventually it did. I made my Neron staff.

And I felt a little more alive.

Then there was the time my Dad broke his arm, and we went into negative credits for the surgery it required. So I made a firing pistol with a Neron core, and I found a buyer.

Immediately, I had plenty of extra credits.

I felt even more alive.

And that was when Reena approached me. Told me about her business, how she could supply the Neron, so I wouldn't get caught by my work. She had a client who had been trying to obtain a Neron weapon from off-planet, but the shipments kept getting intercepted.

I made my second commission then. And I've made dozens more since.

Zayne caught me after a lunar of illegal transactions. To say he was livid was an understatement. He felt…betrayed. Like he didn't know me.

I told him I wasn't going to stop.

When he asked why, I shut down for two solid weeks.

He'd given me space. But again, he asked me why I was doing this. Why I'd gone so far beyond reckless and had stepped into illegal.

I finally broke down and I told him. That I was bored. That I didn't want my life to play out exactly like I could see it happening.

The look in his eyes…I'll never forget it.

He'd begged me to see reason. He made promises, lots of them, to find ways to make life more exciting. We could move to a different part of Korpillion, the other side of the planet. He didn't need to have a child one day—though that was never the problem for me. He would do anything, if I would just stop.

If I would go back to being boring and normal.

I couldn't do it.

So, after weeks of fights, sometimes public ones that were witnessed by half our work, we ended things.

I ended things.

I thought it was going to be the end of my world, because I didn't stop loving Zayne just because I couldn't spend the rest of my life with him. He was my world, and had been for a solar and a half.

After a tense and awkward and very lonely lunar, he approached me in the locker room at work. He finally met my eyes and I looked into his.

And I saw someone I missed.

Someone I'd been dying to talk to.

"Do you want to go laugh at all the stupid drunks at the bar tonight?" he'd hesitantly asked.

Tears filled my eyes as I nodded my head.

We had a talk that night after we laughed at the stupid drunks, about how things weren't going back to what they were. But we both confessed how much we'd missed each other over the past lunar.

And somehow we'd become friends.

They say you can't go back. And maybe someday this will stop working, because I know that Zayne still wants us to be *us*. To have a future of us. But for now, I still have my best friend. And it's a good thing too, because otherwise all I would have is my dad.

I'm not good at…people. I don't like them. I don't let them in. Forming relationships isn't my forte.

I grab the parts on the table, and stick one end in the other. It slides in like a glove.

"Sorry," I say down the mental connection. "I was working earlier. I didn't really feel like looking like a mooned-out psycho in front of my colleague."

"I understand," he immediately responds. "I've had more than a few times where I had to duck into an empty room so I didn't look like I was having…"

"A very serious internal debate with yourself?" I fill in.

I hear him laugh. And I love his laugh. It's simple, and deep. Like it comes from the bottom of his soul, but he keeps it tight and close. He doesn't show it to the world.

"Something like that," he responds.

I slide a rod into the chamber and attach the spring. "Are you anywhere very interesting?"

"I'm actually in a ship somewhere in the T7 sector," he says. My eyebrows raise. He's close. Just a few leagues away from my own sector. "My boss hasn't told me yet where we're heading."

"You're a very adaptable person," I say as I screw on the plate that covers the interworkings.

"Either that or a mindless dog," he says with a little too serious of an undertone.

"I don't think so," I say. "You're snappy and quick and I really can't see you just taking orders from anyone."

"I have my moments of bite when I need to, I suppose."

I press harder on the plate when it refuses to slide into place, which, of course it does, and pinches my finger in the process, drawing blood.

I swear, immediately pressing the injury to my mouth.

"What's wrong?" he demands, concern heavy in his voice.

"Nothing," I groan as I head to the cabinet against the back wall and pull out the first-aid kit Zayne insisted we keep here. It's kind of ridiculous. We work with solid Neron, which could easily obliterate us. Bandages and disinfecting spray aren't going to do much for us here.

But I'm grateful at the moment for them. Not that I'm going to tell Zayne that.

"So, I've been thinking about names that don't start with A or Z," I say, changing the subject.

"And what have you come up with?"

I tape the bandage around my bleeding finger. It's going hurt just as bad tomorrow, I can tell.

"Well, there's Barron," I begin.

"You're kidding, right?" he says with a scoff.

I smile. "There's Vernon."

"Even worse," he says, sounding offended.

"Harrod."

"No."

"Kain?"

"Try again."

I sigh. Really, I have no idea. "Damian."

"I'm only giving you one more guess, and then this game is over," he says. And he actually sounds like he means it.

I shake my head as I return to the worktable, picking up the damaging piece again. "Price."

"No," he immediately says.

"So, game over?" I ask as I finally screw the piece into place.

"Game over," he confirms.

And I smile, because even though it feels like I lost, I'm just glad for the company. The company of someone I can be honest with. Who I can admit all my faults to. Because it's easy when I'm never, ever going to meet the man in my head in real life.

# EIGHT

Early in the morning, I pick up the bag from Crag, and head to the low-level meeting place.

I feel *him* nudge against my brain. But as I see my client up ahead, I shove him out with the thought that I will get back to him later.

Just as the client is transferring the credits to my account, he pushes against my brain again, a little harder this time.

"Not now," I send down the connection, and I shut the door to him.

When the transaction is finished and my account feels nice and padded, I head toward the shop, meeting Zayne part way.

I didn't tell him I was delivering the product this morning. I didn't want him coming. There's no need for him to get mixed up even deeper than he is.

I know he doesn't want to come on deliveries. But he's a chronic worrier, especially when it comes to me.

He lost his parents just after he came of legal age. He'd been in school, staying busy doing what college-aged kids do, partying and drinking too much calypso and working hard in school.

He hadn't thought to check in with his parents. Not for weeks.

When he went home for the holidays, what he found…it wasn't anything anyone should have had to see.

Someone had broken into their cube and killed his family. They'd stolen everything, drained his family'ss accounts. Their bodies hadn't been found for weeks, so the stink and the rot…

I can't entirely blame him for worrying all the time.

Just as we step into the shop, I feel *him* knock at the back door of my brain again.

"I'm obviously busy today!" I yell down the connection. "I'll talk to you tonight."

I get this pressing impression. Of him yelling my name and that he needs to talk to me. But it's as if it's coming from behind a closed door.

"What's on the agenda today?" Zayne asks, grabbing his holotab and pulling up our order list.

We have a battle-axe up next. It's going to be easy and quick, but it also means I can't charge near as much for it.

The smell of molten metal is strong in the air. The forge set us back fifty-thousand credits, but since I don't have access to Horne Energy's anymore, it was a purchase we would have been dead in the water without.

Again, I feel him knock at my brain. But I'm in the middle of pouring the molten steel into the form. I need to concentrate or I'm going to melt my skin right off my bones.

While the metal cools, I set to the handle. I take pride in my work. There's a crystal encasement for the Neron that will be deposited, and some twisting, sculpted steel frames it in a beautiful pattern. I wrap the handle in Tohiri leather.

Together, we grind down the blade, taking it to a sharp point that could slip right down through a man's skull.

I've just attached the blade when my connect-link beeps.

I angle my wrist to my line of sight, activating the screen.

TRANSFER RECEIVED the message displays. THREE MILLION CREDITS DEPOSITED.

My brows furrow and I tap the message, opening it.

"What the void," I mutter under my breath. Sure enough, it is a legitimate alert from my bank. I open up the account, and it displays that I now have three point five million credits.

There are no payment details, and the sender is anonymous.

"What?" Zayne asks as he polishes the blade of the finished axe.

"Someone just-"

But I hear yelling outside. Lots of yelling. They sound absolutely panicked.

Zayne's brows furrow together, and he darts for the main door out the side of the building. I follow him step-for-step. Out in the streets, there are dozens of people, looking up at the sky with gaping mouths, with their hands over their hearts. They shout, their voices terrified-sounding, fingers pointing up.

I turn, stepping further into the street to try and see what they're looking at.

I have to look up, and up, to find the sky above the towering, massive buildings.

But it isn't hard to find or hard to see.

There's a ship in the sky. So large it blots out the sun. So large, it takes up nearly the entire skyline.

It's pitch black, but all of its seams glow brilliant, Neron blue.

There isn't a person in the Eon Galaxy who wouldn't know what that ship was.

*The Dominion.*

Owned by Cyrillius. Used to execute Dominion's business.

It's the ship that ends lives and ruins worlds.

And as I watch, I see a hatch open, and a Class 4 ship smoothly sails out of the Class 1. It's the second most recognizable ship in the galaxy.

*The Black Arrow*. The battleship that belongs to Valen Nero. The last known Nero in the galaxy. The puppet of Cyrillius.

"No," the word slips over my lips as my heart turns cold.

Dominion has come. The end is already here.

And I'm still on Korpillion.

I was supposed to have four more solars. I was supposed to be gone in three. We were supposed to be settled and comfortable on Panus long before this day came. Long before that ship blotted out the sky.

The name Dominion ripples throughout the air. Gasps, and tears, and shouted plans ripple through the street.

I can't feel my heart. I don't feel a beat in my chest, I can't hear pounding in my ears.

My wrist vibrates and numbly, I raise it to activate the screen. There's a message there, but no sender name.

*21908 Airspace 21, Hangar 15.*

My brows furrow, confusion ripping through my chest like a hurricane mixed with my panic.

"Who is that from?" Zayne asks, looking down at the message I'm trying to make sense of.

"I have no idea," I say, shaking my head. "There is no sender. How is that even possible?"

"It isn't that difficult to hide that information," Zayne says.

"Why are they sending you an address at the Airspace?"

"Zayne, someone also just dumped three million credits into my account," I say as my eyes rise up to meet his.

I feel this...pit in my stomach. There's something cold and heavy in the bottom of it.

"Come on," I say, grabbing his wrist and dragging him back into the shop. "We've got to get out of here."

"Where the void are we going to go, Nova?" he says, even though he whips around the space, gathering his things.

"Well, I've got the credits to get us off Korpillion now," I say. I grab my cargo bag from a shelf, double check my staff is inside. I grab a few tools. I don't know why, but I feel handicapped without them. I grab my own holotab and stuff it in. And last, I grab the battle-axe and squeeze it into the bag. It barely fits. But it fits. "Whoever is doing this seems to want to get me off the planet. We have to go to the Airspace and see what's waiting for me in that hangar."

There's a look of panic and stress in his eyes, but Zayne nods. His eyes sweep the shop one last time, making sure we have everything, and we walk out of the shop.

It hurts me a little bit. I'd just gotten established. I've worked so hard for this. And now I have to walk away from everything that made me *me* on this planet.

"Let's go," I say, grabbing Zayne's hand, and darting down the walkway that weaves through the buildings. Where the streets should have been somewhat cleared right now while everyone is inside working, they're packed as more and more realize that something is happening outside and they go to see the doom that is coming for them.

We're not the only ones racing somewhere, though. Others dart through the skywalks, heading wherever seems safer, heading to meet their loved ones. But there will be no escape for the vast majority of them.

Dad's school is two and a half kilometers from my warehouse. With how crowded the streets are, it's almost impossible to move faster than a walk.

But suddenly, the masses come to a dead stop.

There's movement in the sky.

*The Black Arrow* exited *The Dominion*, and just hovered in the sky, as if waiting for orders. But now it lights up blue, and sails forward, smooth and silent. All eyes stop and watch as it descends.

There is a government building just one block from our old work. Between the two, there is the only flat, mid-Terra level space in the whole city. There are fountains and gardens there and the only four trees left on the entire planet. There's a tiny patch of grass. It's supposed to serve as a reminder of what the planet once was. The only green space for millions and millions of kilometers.

*The Black Arrow* descends and I know the green space is exactly where it lands.

I swear, tugging on Zayne's wrist once more, and take off down the skywalk.

This is bad. So bad.

Dad's school is right across from that park where The Black Arrow is landing.

Just then, *The Dominion's* hatch opens once more, and a dozen Class 5 ships spill out of it, heading in three different directions.

Oh, void.

"Someone must have talked," Zayne says as we race through the skywalks. "I knew there were too many rumors going around about on-planet Neron."

It's just a constant stream of swear words going through my head.

What if this is my fault? For exposing my staff a few weeks ago? What if someone questioned where I got the Neron? What if they wanted to make a few credits for telling Dominion about all the rumors, and then the confirmation that they'd seen an activated Neron weapon on a supposedly Neron-less planet?

The school comes into view, but there is no back entry. We have to round the entire block to get to the doors. My heart is hammering in my throat at the thought of having to get so close to *The Black Arrow*, but I have no other option.

As we close in on the corner of the building, I slow, pressing my back flat to the building. Slowly, I peer around the corner.

The Square is silent. Not a soul occupies the normally crowded space. *The Black Arrow* fills the entire space, except the great stairs that rise up to the park. I see the debris of the last four trees on Korpillion, crushed and splintered beneath the weight of the ship.

The hatch of the ship hasn't opened yet. I don't see anyone around. I don't have any time to waste, so I grab Zayne and drag him along the front of the building, sprinting for the front doors of the school.

There are terrified whimpers and muttered regrets when we walk inside. All of the children have their noses pressed to the glass, staring wide-eyed and terrified at the Nero's ship.

But I can't think about them right now. I have to find my father, and I have to get us off this planet.

We dart through the halls and I immediately head toward the stairs at the back of the building. Down we go, down, down, three floors until we're at Terra level where it's dark and smells of equipment and grease.

"Dad?" I yell, looking up and down the service hallways. "Dad, where are you?"

"Nova?" I hear him call from back, deep in the tunnels.

I run that direction. "Dad, come on. We have to get out of here."

He steps out into the hall, and I collide with him, chest to chest. He grabs me, staining my arms with his greased hands. His gray eyes stare into mine, searching for the reason for my panic.

"What's going on?" he asks. There's a hint of fear in his voice. Because I don't spook easily, and he can see the fear in my eyes.

"Dominion is here," I say the words very clearly and calm. "They brought their ship, and their soldiers, and even the Nero is here with *The Black Arrow*."

Torin's eyes widen, fear and confusion filling them. "Why?" he questions. "Why would they ever come here?"

"Because there *is* Neron on Korpillion," Zayne fills in.

I watch as terror fills my father's face. I swear, I can see his entire life flashing before his eyes. His grip on my arms tightens, to the point I wince in pain.

"We have to go," he says in a breathy whisper. "We have to get off this planet."

I nod in agreement. He doesn't know I now have the means to do that. But he understands. He knows what will happen if we stay.

He doesn't even grab anything. He has nothing to take. He's a lowly maintenance worker that doesn't even have claim to the tools he uses down here in the dark to keep this building functioning for the future of Korpillion.

But there is no future here, anymore.

Together, the three of us dash back up the stairs. As we near the doors, we slow though.

Because it's absolutely quiet in the school now.

All the teachers and all the students are still standing with their faces pressed to the glass. But they don't make a sound now. They barely breathe.

We walk up to those front doors with their glass windows, and look outside at how the view of the park has changed.

Two-dozen Dominion soldiers stand in the park, their Neron weapons pointed at eleven people on their knees.

# NINE

There are four women and one man dressed in shredded, dangling black clothing. Their fingertips are withered and black. Black also creeps out from their mouths, like half a dozen enormous spiders are trying to escape their mouths, but only the legs have emerged from their lips.

And their eyes. Solid black. Soulless. The things of nightmares.

The Kinduri.

A man stands before the prisoners on their knees. Anyone would recognize him from the holo reports. He's the richest, most powerful man in the galaxy. Cyrillius.

And beside him, dressed in solid black, standing far taller than any of the others, with his black mask on, is none other then Valen Nero.

My heart stops. The scene is bad. It's terrifying, and it's the opening act of what is to come, to what our world is about to evolve into.

But it's not what stops the blood from flowing through my veins.

It's that I know those eleven people on their knees with their hands behind their heads. I recognize every one of their faces.

They're Reena's workers. The miners. The preparers. Every person who assists Reena in running the Neron mine is there on their knees. And I know what is about to become of them.

But as I scan their faces for the tenth time, I confirm. Reena is not among them.

I know what happened. Dominion's soldiers used their scanners to find the mine. They found all the workers doing their jobs. They took them, brought them here.

Reena had to have been out on a deal.

And it saved her life.

A crowd has gathered around the Square, watching with terror and fear. The Regulator of Korpillion stands out on the government stairs, his affiliates with him. They watch with solemn faces, because they know there isn't a slam thing they can do now that Dominion is here.

Cyrillius turns and his eyes scan the crowd. Not only looking at those who stand outside, watching and waiting, but they sweep the buildings, as if he can see the millions of people who surround him.

"Dominion offers you its greetings."

I press my hands over my ears, because suddenly, they're vibrating with the sound of Cyrillius' voice.

Every building on the planet is soundproofed. It's the only way to stay sane on a planet with twenty-eight point one billion noise creators.

But I feel the vibrations of sound everywhere. Beneath my feet, as if its traveling through the steel frames of the buildings. I feel it coming off the walls.

I don't know how he does it, but I feel his words, right in my chest as if he's pounding them right into my heart.

"I know that you are afraid," Cyrillius says. He's calm; he actually looks peaceful as his eyes sweep the crowd. "I know there are stories and accounts from other worlds. But Dominion is not what you need fear."

I shake my head.

I've heard of his lies. Arden Black has broadcasted interviews with the man before. But actually hearing them live, from his own lips, I want to *end* him.

"Chaos is what you should fear," Cyrillius continues. "Disorder is what you should fear. I want you to imagine it. A galaxy where there is no one to regulate Neron. A galaxy where Neron may be claimed by anyone. Any army. Any government. I want you to imagine a galaxy where Neron is used in interplanetary warfare."

I don't want to imagine what he's saying, but I can't help it.

And for just a second, I believe it.

I can imagine a galaxy where Neron is under free claim.

I can imagine the wars. The destruction. The entire planets that could be obliterated.

But I shake my head. I know what Dominion has done with their self-obtained power. I know the trillions of lives they've altered. The mothers and fathers and children they've turned into slaves and then killed.

I know what they did to the people on Hogwa just days ago.

"I know that Dominion's presence is taxing on a planet," Cyrillius says. His voice is gentle, understanding. He sounds like a father talking to his children. "But the galaxy would turn into a wasteland without it."

"Shut your lying slag mouth," Zayne says under his breath.

I look around. I forgot I was surrounded by children and teachers. I want to put my hands over their ears, so they can't hear the lies Cyrillius tells so well. I want them to turn away from the window so they can't see the caring look on his face.

They don't know any better.

They don't know the truth.

"For the safety of the galaxy," Cyrillius says, his voice magically amplified to fill the city, "we must bring those individuals who selfishly kept Korpillion's Neron to themselves to justice."

"Look away," I hear the teachers say. "Come away from the windows," they frantically instruct.

A few of the students listen, but most can't tear their eyes away.

I can't either.

I watch in horror.

The Kinduri step forward, placing their hands on either side of the miner's heads. Their own heads turn skyward, their black eyes sliding closed. The miners seem frozen and their mouths fall open as if they are in excruciating pain, but no sound escapes.

One by one, each of the miners is touched by a Kinduri. I think I know what they're doing. I think they're pulling information from those miners' heads.

Eating Neron grants you certain gifts. It curses you. Makes you into…what they are. But it gives you abilities.

Like the ability to steal thoughts from people's heads.

Like the ability to find my face inside those miner's heads.

My heart is thundering in my chest. My palms are slick with sweat.

They're going to find my face in the memories of those miners. They've seen me at the mine. They know how I work with Reena.

And now the Kinduri have Reena's face, as well.

One by one, the Kinduri go to Cyrillius, whispering words in his ear, their black lips moving, sealing my fate.

When they're finished, they stand behind their master.

Cyrillius stands tall and straight. He rolls his shoulders back, but there's a new tightness to them.

"A reward," he says, his voice loud and clear. "For the head or capture of Reena McDyer, the woman who put this entire planet at risk."

My heart thunders as he says her name. My palms are slick with sweat.

A reward, for her head. Cyrillius wants Reena, dead or alive.

"And a reward, for the capture of the weapons maker," Cyrillius says, sealing my fate.

Zayne's eyes snap to me. But I can't look away. I'm frozen, rooted. A terrified, frozen corpse of a wanted woman.

Cyrillius steps forward. He folds his hands behind his back.

He's all angles. His head is covered with russet colored hair, his tanned face splashed with freckles and imperfections. He bears a proud nose and a square chin.

He's a washed out hue of brown, all over. He should be forgettable, but his eyes are so cold, and his very presence is so commanding, no one would ever forget Cyrillius.

"We cannot allow individuals to put our beautiful Eon Galaxy at risk," he says. "Dominion's presence is taxing, but the reward is peace."

My name. The miners never knew my name.

I breathe a sigh of relief.

My eyes were so focused on Cyrillius at first that I did not even realize what was happening until some of the children call out in awe, pointing at the Nero.

The air around his left hand is glowing blue, and more strands of glowing blue float through the air in electric arc's that dance and spark.

It's incredible.

Neron is everywhere. It's in the air. It's in every material we used to build this sprawling city planet.

The Nero can pull it out of anything.

They can wield it however they want.

I watch Valen Nero's hand, and see the Neron flattening out into a long, pointed object. Like a spear.

"No," I breathe as my blood turns cold. I clutch my bag tighter to myself, needing something to hold onto. Something to keep me grounded.

"We must maintain peace, for the galaxy." Cyrillius turns back to the miners.

The Nero gives one flick of his hand. And the spear launches so fast, my eyes can't even track it.

It rockets forward, seemingly passing right in front of all those miners.

But as the Neron spear immediately dissipates, the miner closest to Valen Nero suddenly folds to the ground. Followed by the next, and then the next. One by one, all eleven of those miners' bodies collapse to the ground.

Screams from the children rip through the building as little lines of blood leak from the sides of each of the miner's heads.

The Nero shot the spear through all eleven of their heads. Without any effort. Without any thought.

Now they all lie there—dead.

The Nero killed them, and Cyrillius didn't bat an eye.

All because they were using the Neron he has now laid a claim to.

My stomach is sick. I have to turn away for a minute, leaning my forehead on my father's shoulder as I take five slow breaths. I'm scared. I feel ill. I can't think.

*Get out of here*, a voice says in my head, the voice of logic. *There's nothing you can do. You can't help anyone. Save yourself and the ones you care about.*

I take two more deep breaths. And then I set my bag down on the ground and unzip it.

My fingers wrap around the handle of the axe. I pause like that for several long moments, staring at the Neron core I placed inside the crystal encasement just moments before the world ended.

It's all changed now.

My life, my world will never be the same.

And I'm so slam ready.

I lift the axe and my eyes rise to see my father looking at me with absolute shock and horror in his eyes. I extend it toward him.

"Getting off this planet isn't going to be easy," I say. I hope he listens to me, every single syllable. I hope he feels them in his bones, in his heart, in his blood. "But I'm going to do whatever it takes to get us out of here. You can chew me out later, but right now, we have to do what needs to be done."

And maybe I don't know my father as well as I thought I did. He's horrified, because now he knows: I'm the one that Cyrillius himself said he wants brought to him. But my father's eyes harden. The set of his lips thin out. And he reaches out and wraps his fingers around the handle and holds it with a confidence I never would have assumed in a million solars.

Zayne understands, because as I take my staff out, he removes his hilt from his own bag.

I dig into mine, and find the bottle of black smudge.

"The Kinduri might not have found my name, but they have my face now," I explain as I unscrew the lid and dip two of my fingers in it. I draw a line from my hairline, across my brows, to the other side of my hair. I fill it in beneath my eyes until a thick, dark band masks my face. "For all I know, they might have yours, too, Zayne."

I stand, dipping my fingers into the smudge. I draw a line straight down his face, dividing it in half. I fill in the left side of his face until it is entirely black.

"And I won't risk anyone recognizing you either, Dad," I say, turning to him. I make an upside down V, with the tip of it starting right between his eyes. I fill the lower part of it in solid.

We look like warriors. Not prey trying to escape.

We need any extra boost of confidence we can get right now.

A scream rips through this level of the school, followed by another. My heart explodes in my throat as I turn back to the scene outside.

Those locals who had gathered, who just witnessed that scene, have swarmed the Square. And they're fighting.

They're only throwing trash and a few of them actually have hand weapons that fire metal and spikes.

But it's a slaughter.

Dominion's armies carry the most advanced Neron weapons in the galaxy. They obliterate the locals who are only reacting to injustice. They literally blow them to unidentifiable pieces.

My mouth opens and a soundless scream slips out into the world.

This is it. This is how Korpillion goes the way of all the other Neron worlds before it.

"Come on," Zayne says, stooping to help me zip up my bag. "We have to find a way out of here."

"This way," Dad says, grabbing my wrist and tugging me back toward the back end of the school. We dart past dozens of classrooms, all filled with terrified children and teachers who could never be qualified to handle a planetary takeover.

At the back of the school, we come to a restroom. Against the outside wall, there is a large, frosted glass window that lets in the little natural light that makes it down this far.

"It doesn't open," Zayne says, searching the frame of it for a way to open it wide enough for us to slip out.

I press the activating button on my staff as I thrust it forward. The arc juts forward, connecting with the glass, and shatters it. I sweep it around the frame of the window, clearing all the jagged glass.

Not wasting another second, I deactivate my staff, clipping it onto my belt, and climb through, careful to avoid the shards on the ground. Zayne and my father immediately follow. And just behind them is a whole mess of children.

I send out a prayer to the galaxy that they can make it home to their families unharmed. Children are innocent. They shouldn't get caught up in Dominion's greed.

"This way," Zayne says, reaching for my free hand and tugging us back the way we just came. Together, the three of us run, hand in hand, down the skywalks, and then turn left down a sidewalk. My lungs are tired; my legs are exhausted. My heart screams at me to calm down.

But we keep running, turning down street after street.

We burst through the front door of our cube and I slam it shut behind us.

"We need food," I say, immediately going to the kitchen. We don't keep a large stockpile here for just the two of us, but I dump every non-perishable item we have into my huge bag. I yell at Zayne to start filling water containers, as much as we can carry.

I dart into my bedroom and grab a few changes of clothes, my extra pair of boots. I stuff those in the already full bag.

Dad emerges from his bedroom with his own bag.

I look around the tiny home that we have shared for forever. We don't own anything of value. There's nothing else worth taking.

"Do you need to go back to your cube?" I ask Zayne.

He grabs my bag, shouldering it. "Nothing worth grabbing."

"Let's get going," Torin says. He opens the door wide, and Zayne and I shuffle out.

We're two kilometers from the Airstrip. My legs are already tired. I feel like I've been running all over the city today. I'm used to walking everywhere, but nothing like this. Not under these circumstances.

The world is always noisy, but it was taken to an entirely new level today.

I hear shots being fired. Shots from Neron weapons and Korpillion ones. I hear screams. Class 6 ships zip around the sky now, and I hope and pray that they are only doing surveillance and not getting ready to fire on anyone.

The most direct path to the Airspace takes us within three blocks of the Square. Logic tells me to take a longer route, to steer clear of ground zero.

But there's no time.

I'm already tired.

I don't see any other choice but to take the fastest route.

"We'll be to the Airspace in ten minutes," I huff. I reach back, grabbing my father's hand as he lags behind. I tug him faster, and he picks up the pace.

I hear a boom. And then another. It's followed by the sound of falling debris and the ground shakes.

It sounded ten blocks away. Like a building beginning to collapse. My fear doubles.

Nearly every building on Korpillion is over fifty stories high. If one falls, it could cause a domino effect that could never stop until it reaches the coast.

"Come on!" Zayne yells, looking over his shoulder. I can't believe how fast he still is, considering he's carrying my loaded bag, plus his own.

"Dad, give me your bag," I say through my panting breath. "We need to move faster."

He gives me this growl that says *no way in void I'm going to make my daughter carry my bag.* But he picks up the pace and Zayne slows down to let us catch up.

There's another boom. I hear screams rip through the sky. One of the Class 6 ships shoots over our heads, sending my hair wild and in my face. A moment later, I hear another boom.

A woman crashes into me from the right, the crowd is so chaotic and panicked. She sends me sailing to my side, knocking me underfoot in the crowd. I barely manage to keep hold of my staff.

Someone tramples over me, stepping on my stomach, the toe of their boot catching my chin, which cracks my head back against the skywalk. A startled, painful yelp rips from my chest. I roll to my side, pushing myself up, climbing back to my feet.

The skywalk is packed with frantic people who don't really know where they're going, but they feel like they have to be doing something. There are thousands of bodies packed around me, all in this little space.

I can't see my dad. I can't see Zayne.

All I see is thousands of unfamiliar faces.

There's another boom, and it's so loud, it makes my ears ring and I swear they're bleeding.

And then there's a cracking sound. A million pops. Glass shatters.

And the building just up ahead instantly crumbles. It tips. It shatters.

It falls. Right where our group had been running before I fell.

"Dad!" I scream. I take two steps forward, but a huge chunk of concrete lands just four feet in front of me, followed by a pouring rain of shattered glass.

I watch as hundreds of people are shredded by it.

"Zayne!"

And the world in front of me grows dark.

The towering building falls sideways. The top of it hits the next building, shattering glass, making an explosion that rains down on us below. The ground shakes at the impact. But it does not fall.

But the first, it collapses to the street with a thunderous clap.

And all those people in front of me, the hundreds and hundreds of people in the shadow of that building, they're just gone. They disappear beneath the debris.

I'm stuck for a moment. A scream is lodged somewhere in my throat. But it can't find it's way past my horror.

Dad. Zayne.

# TEN

My ears finally process sound once more, and the air is filled with screams, with mourning, angry cries. There are frantic calls of pain. There are hundreds around me who are injured.

And I stand here, just twenty feet from where a massive building just collapsed, and I don't have more than a scratch on my left forearm and a scrape across my right cheek.

"Nova!" I hear a frantic yell coming from my wrist.

And emotion instantly springs in my eyes. I raise my wrist up, hearing Zayne's frantic screaming.

"I'm here!" I yell back. "I'm here. Are you both okay?"

I hear his relieved breath through the connect-link. "We were just on the other side of the building when it came down. We didn't realize you were gone."

"I was pushed over," I say, so relieved. I thought they were dead. I really thought they were both gone and that I was instantly alone. "I'm okay."

"Stay where you are," he says. "We'll come find you."

"No," I say, shaking my head. I break out of my freeze, making my feet move again. "We don't have time. You two keep heading to the Airspace. I will meet you there in just a few minutes."

"Nova, I-"

"Just do it, Zayne!" I yell at him. "I'm a big slam girl. I'll meet you there in just a few."

I hang up on him so I don't have to hear either of them arguing with me.

I head toward the foundation of the building to cut around it and get back on the path to the Airspace. I pick my way through the debris. I tell myself not to think as I step over bodies. I go into survival mode because there's blood all around me, the destruction everywhere.

The sounds of shooting get farther away, heading in the opposite direction, even though the Square is only two blocks from here. I hear the sounds of thousands of feet making their retreat, desperate to find somewhere safe.

I round the block, hoping to find a clear path, but I find heaps of debris stretching out in either direction.

I have no choice but to climb up and over it.

Tucking my staff into my tunic, I hoist myself up the first boulder of concrete and twisted steel. I grab a bar sticking out of it, pulling myself up. Carefully, I climb over the twisted support beams. Thankfully, all the glass seems to have filtered down through the concrete, trying to find its way to the ground below.

I crest the top of the heap. Looking down, I see more and more piles of debris. And no one in sight, except for those crushed by the buildings.

The end. It's the end of Korpillion. It's the end for that woman lying with her face crushed to the street. It's the end for whoever is attached to that arm sticking out from beneath that steel beam. It's the end for whoever belonged to that shoe lying alone.

There are a million emotions ripping through me. But the strongest ones are hate and grief.

*He* was right. I do miss the boring and the predictable. I'd give anything to have it back, to rewind twenty-seven hours. I hated my life, and I didn't appreciate the safety.

I begin working my way down the heap, determined that I have to get to the Airstrip. The boulders are unstable and metal groans under the pressure I put on the heap. Everything I'm climbing over is unstable. It could shift and twist and trap me in the mess.

A chunk of concrete rolls as I step on it and I lose my grounding, my right ankle gets caught between something as my left leg rolls forward with the debris. I twist, trying to keep my balance. My hand flings out, darting to catch myself. But it connects with the sharp end of a steel rod, and the tip of it sinks into my flesh, and my eyes widen in horror as I see the very tip of it appear on the back of my hand.

A stifled scream escapes my lips as I squeeze my eyes closed.

*Think, Nova,* I try to calm myself. *You have to get yourself out of here. You have to go find Torin and Zayne and get off this planet. And then you can cry and scream.*

Gritting my teeth, I rip my hand away from the steel, immediately pressing it to my chest to keep it from bleeding any more than necessary. With only my right hand, I brace myself, and pull my ankle free.

But the whole mountain of debris suddenly breaks and settles, and I'm falling, bouncing down the pile, hitting concrete and steel, until I land at the bottom.

And my eyes widen as I see three huge boulders smashing and bouncing their way down the same path I just came.

They head directly toward me, and I know I don't stand a chance at moving out of their way.

Preparing for the impact, I hold my hands above myself, my fingers splayed wide, and I wait to be crushed.

There is one last great crack as the boulders roll and then bounce down the mountain of rubble, and then silence.

I wait. And wait, my face cringed, waiting for a second of pain before it's all over.

But it doesn't come.

It's silent.

I dare crack my eyelids open.

But they immediately flash wide open in disbelief.

Above me, directly above my outstretched hands, is a glowing blue disk, three of them actually. Floating above the disks, as if supported, are the three huge boulders that would have meant my death.

But they hover there. Blocked. Held back.

By Neron.

A curse slips from my lips in a huff.

I move my hands, swinging them to the left a little, and the boulders swing over at the same time.

"No," I breathe. "Not…not possible."

But I shift them even further, and the Neron answers me, moving the boulders.

"Nova?"

A voice startles my attention back to reality, and instantly the Neron dissipates and the boulders crash to the ground, just a foot from where I lie.

A figure steps into the pit of the debris. A figure dressed in black. A figure with a mask.

But his voice... The way he said my name...

I instantly scramble to my feet, wincing because every single part of my body screams in pain. I grab my staff from my tunic, eternally grateful that it didn't get dislodged in my fall.

"I heard you," he says, and my insides shrivel. I turn cold. "Screaming in my head. And I felt...you, here."

The air is very still. I'm entirely frozen.

No.

No.

"What are you still doing here?" the Nero asks as he takes a step forward.

I've seen images of the Nero before, I would recognize his uniform anywhere. Anyone in the galaxy would.

But I have never heard him speak.

His voice is deep, piercing. Unlike any voice I have ever heard before.

"I tried to warn you, to tell you to leave the planet," he says from behind his mask. "Why are you not on that ship?"

Emotions rip through me.

Elation. And terror.

"You shouldn't still be here, Nova."

I pull in my lower lip in an attempt to control the emotions that want to pour out of me. My hands shake, barely able to keep a grip on my staff. Blood drips from my left hand, pooling on the sidewalk below my feet.

"You?" I ask with a quiver in my voice.

He stands very still. The broad set to his shoulders hardly even rises and falls with his breath. His eyes are locked on me, even though I can't see them through his mask.

"It's *you?*" I ask. My voice is very quiet and threatens to crack.

He takes a step forward, and another, and I react automatically. I activate my staff and both arcs dart out, crackling in the air as I take a defensive stance, holding it up between him and me.

He hesitates, observing me with the staff. But he must not feel threatened, because he takes two more steps forward before stopping, only ten feet between us.

He reaches up, and he removes his mask.

For lunars, I've wondered what he would look like. I confided in him. He's been in my head, learning intimate details about me. And here he is.

I know it. I can't deny it.

Valen Nero is the man I've been talking to all this time.

His jaw is narrow and long, his cheekbones sharp and defined. Black hair falls wild around his face, his brows just as black.

He stares out at me with eyes as blue as the Neron he wields.

He's beautiful.

But this is the face of *Valen Nero*. Puppet of Cyrillius, of Dominion.

He killed all those miners in the Square. He killed all those people on Hogwa. And I know he's killed hundreds, maybe thousands, before them.

"No," I say as emotion cracks my voice.

"Nova," he says, his voice a breath, and the way he says my name...

I shake my head, wanting to collapse, to capsize on myself. I can't handle anymore. It is all too much.

But I make myself stand tall, ignore the blood spilling from my hand, and hold onto my Neron staff.

"I saw what you did," he says, his eyes darting to the boulders I'd somehow kept from crushing me. "Did you know?"

A tear pushes its way out onto my cheek but I shake my head furiously. "I know nothing. I *am* nothing."

Valen shakes his head, his eyes so intense I feel like he can read every one of my thoughts. And I guess he can.

"It makes sense now, why we formed the connection," he says. I can tell, he wants to come closer. But he doesn't. Because he can see the anger and the betrayal rolling off of me in waves. "I've heard stories about it happening. That telepathic bonds could form between two Ner-"

"I am nothing!" I scream. "I am the daughter of a powerless

maintenance worker. I am a wanted weapons manufacturer and dealer. I…am…nothing!"

Valen takes one step forward, shaking his head just twice, with absolute conviction. "You're not nothing, Nova."

More tears work their way out onto my face. My heart has expanded to the size of my entire chest and it beats so painfully strong.

I didn't even realize it at first, but there are glowing blue particles swirling around my legs. They work their way up my torso, then to my arms. Just tiny little blue flecks in the air. Gently, they land on my body, and they disappear into my skin.

A breath of relief escapes my lips as the pain disappears. It evaporates. I feel my body healing, all the little cracks in my bones, the ruptured blood vessels. The puncture in my hand.

I don't even see him doing anything, but Valen pulls the Neron from the air and sends it to heal me.

I shake my head, feeling like I'm going to shatter with all the emotions rearranging my organs.

"You need to leave, Nova," Valen says, taking one more step forward. "The Kinduri have your face. They're looking for you, and the woman who was running the mine. If they find you, Cyrillius will use you and then kill you."

He takes another step forward, and the Neron arc of my staff illuminates his face.

Why does he have to be so beautiful?

"You have to get off this planet, Nova," Valen says. He takes another step forward. If he comes any closer, the arc will cut right through him and even a Nero can't survive that.

But he reaches up, his hand coming up beneath my staff and my arms. I should be more vigilant, but my eyes slide closed, just for a moment, when his fingertips touch my cheekbone and his thumb brushes over my lips just once.

I'm frozen. Rooted. I feel as if I've just fallen, fallen far and deep down a dark pit.

My eyes slide open, but everything is different.

I'm looking at…myself. And Valen.

I stand beside him, wearing a dark, black gown, the finest thing I've ever seen. Some kind of black crown sits atop my head, woven into my blonde hair.

And Valen…  He's dressed similarly. He wears regal black clothes. A black crown sits atop his head. And it's the most natural sight in the world.

Behind us, a planet burns. There are cries of grief and terror floating through the air.

But neither of us seem to notice it.

Valen looks down at me with absolute intent, and…peace.

I know that look in his eyes. It's love.

I'm looking up at him, and not a piece of me doubts that is adoration in my own eyes. That is devotion.

That is love.

Between our two bodies, our hands are together, fingers interlaced.

Valen raises his other hand, bringing it to the side of my neck.

That vision of me leans forward, her eyes sliding closed. Her hand comes up to rest on Valen's chest.

Love.

So much love.

I lean in closer, and I'm holding my breath as the space between our lips becomes smaller and smaller.

The wind shifts, and my eyes fly open.

Destruction is all around me. But just a breath away, Valen's lips are hovering just in front of mine.

My blood-covered hand is on his chest. My staff is deactivated, in the other.

Valen's hand is on the side of my neck, holding me so close, so tender.

I meet his Neron blue eyes, and the shock, the confusion, the grief in his eyes tells me he saw something, too.

I jerk away from him, but it feels as if my heart just fractured into a dozen different pieces.

I shake my head. I back up four steps.

I activate my staff once more, holding it up between us.

"I will come for you, Nova," Valen breathes.

I study those Neron blue eyes, wondering if his words are a promise or a threat. And my heart doesn't know which one it should be.

I nearly cry out in protest when he steps away and immediately replaces his mask. I can't… I need…

What just happened?

What was that?

Who was I?

Valen takes five steps toward the mountain blocking my path and extends his hand.

Neron instantly glows in and around every bit of the debris, shifting and rearranging, until there is a clear path back in the direction I need to go to get to the Airspace.

"Get off this planet," the Nero says. "Don't ever return to Korpillion."

I straighten, my eyes flicking between the pathway and the Nero. I hesitate.

I have a million things I need to say, a thousand questions to ask.

"Go, Nova!" he suddenly yells.

It breaks me out of my frozen trance. My feet move. And with my eyes still frozen on his black mask, I run.

# ELEVEN

I dart. I race. I dash down the path Valen created with the magic he wields, his control over Neron. I deactivate my staff so I don't accidentally injure myself.

But I only get twenty yards away when a figure leaps out from the shadow of an abandoned building. They grab me by the tunic, ripping me around, and then pinning me to the side of a building.

Reena.

"You have a way off this planet, and I am coming with you," she hisses in my face. Her eyes are wild, manic. Terrified.

But determined.

"They have your name," I say. I'm not sure if I'm even making any sense, if the words come out right. My brain is reeling. Too much. Too much.

"The Kinduri have our faces," I breathe. "I was worried they'd find you."

"You have a ship," Reena says. And the focused, hard way she says the words, I know she knows. She saw. She heard. Everything that just happened with Valen. "Get me off this planet." Wildly, she searches my eyes, begging. "Please."

She knows.

She saw.

I can't let Reena stay here and die, and I know I don't have a choice but to agree.

She could out me, for so many things.

"Let go of me so we can get out of here," I say, pushing her off of me.

And together we run. We run and run, for what feels like forever, the remaining kilometer to the Airspace.

I know we're getting close, because I see dozens of ships taking off. They litter the sky. They fill the air with the scent of burned oxygen. They rise and disappear into the solar system as their Neron cores illuminate the world and then propel them to places far away from here.

And there are the crowds.

There has to be tens of thousands of people here. They're pressing in on the gates, they're climbing the fences. They're sobbing and begging.

The guards at the Airspace stand there, holding their weapons. They look conflicted. They look tortured. They don't know what to do. They know these people will likely die if they stay here; we've already seen that in the two hours since Dominion arrived.

But they have a job to do. And there are not near enough ships to get them off-planet.

A message vibrates my wrist. It's from Zayne.

CUT EAST ALONG THE MAIN GATE. TURN LEFT AT THE ZELLOS BUILDING. THE HANGARS ARE ALONG THAT ROAD. NO CROWDS.

"Come on," I say, nodding my head to Reena.

We fight our way through the crowd along the fence. Thankfully it grows thinner in the half kilometer we run to find the Zellos building. And finally, there it is.

The shouting echoes through the road we cut down, but there are no crowds here. A quarter of a kilometer down, I see two figures standing off to the side of the road.

"Holy stars above," my father says as I jog up to him. He pulls me into his arms, hugging me tight to him, burying his face in my neck. "I was so scared when we got separated. Are you alright?"

"I'm fine," I say as he releases me and looks me over. And I *am* fine. I feel great. Amazing.

Because Valen healed me with Neron.

"So, you made it out of whatever hole you were hiding in?" Zayne says with spite in his voice.

All eyes fall on Reena. "I'm not ready to die today," she says in that haughty, elegant way of hers. But she doesn't meet Zayne's or my father's eyes.

"She's coming with us," I say, stating it simply.

We might not exactly like each other's company, even if I only don't like her because she doesn't like me, but she's one of the only people I associate with on the planet, I'm not just going to leave her when I know for a fact that Dominion is hunting for her and will kill her the second she's found.

"What's going on?" I move on. "Is this the address of the hanger? Have you gone in to see what's in there?"

They both shake their heads. "The message was sent to you," Zayne says. "We thought it was better if you were the one to walk in there."

I nod.

There's a door there. I double-check it with the address. I realize now that it was Valen who sent me the message. And put all the credits into my account.

He kept trying to connect with me today to warn me.

*My boss hasn't told me yet where we're going.*

He'd been in the T sector. He'd been on his way here when we'd last spoken.

Did he really not know he was on his way to Korpillion? It wouldn't have been hard for him to figure out I was here on this planet. There aren't any others around that don't belong to Dominion.

*Stop*, I yell at myself. *You can think everything over a million times later. Right now, just get off this doomed planet.*

I step forward, and twist the doorknob. It opens, and I step through.

Dim lights turn on at my movement.

It's a medium-sized hangar, fairly standard. Sitting in the center of it is a Class 5 ship. They're typically transport ships, with a command deck, small living quarters and a mechanical room. They're big enough to transport five or six people to wherever you might want to go.

And standing just to the side of the ship, is a Frank.

They're actually FR's—function robots. They're programmed to do one specific kind of job, and not much else. They are somewhat human-shaped, with chunky torsos and blocky heads. They have long skinny legs and long dangling arms.

When we walk in, the lights where its eyes would be if it were human light up as it activates. It takes two steps forward.

"Welcome, Nova," it says in a smooth but mechanical voice. "I am ready to pilot you off Korpillion. Please board *The Corsair*." It extends its arm, and the hatch of the ship opens, revealing a ramp.

Zayne and Torin both look at me, the same question in their eyes. *Who? Why?*

But we have to leave right now.

We all climb into the ship, and the Frank tromps its way up the ramp.

There's a pilot's seat where all the controls are, and a copilot seat beside it. There are four other seats behind it.

Zayne takes the copilot seat. It's been his dream to become a pilot. But with so many people on this planet, the competition for the few positions there are was too steep. He didn't make it through the program, so instead, he studied information systems.

I sit in the seat behind the Frank, my father in the seat beside me, and Reena takes one of the last-row seats.

"Give me your connect-link," Zayne says, tapping something on his own. "We can't have anyone tracking us."

I extend my arm to him and he taps it, making it beep and information flashes between my screen to his and then back again. He does it with Reena and Torin's, hiding our signals and information.

The Frank doesn't push buttons or tap on the multitude of screens. A port extends from his fingers, plugging right into the ship. There's a soft hum as the engine starts and it lifts off the ground.

The doors to the hangar open, revealing the chaotic Airspace.

"What planet would you like me to input as our destination, Nova?" the Frank asks.

Everyone looks at me.

Panus was my plan. We were going to be safe there and we could start a new life.

But now that everything has ended, now that everything has changed, it doesn't feel right.

"I don't know," I answer honestly. I shake my head, wishing everyone would stop looking at me like I'm in charge and know what the void I'm doing. "Just get us out of this solar system. We'll figure the rest out later."

The Frank doesn't make any noise of acknowledgement, but the ship smoothly sails forward. Through the hangars we make our way and line up in the departure lane.

There are hundreds of other ships waiting their turn to escape Korpillion.

And for just a second, I make myself marvel over this moment.

I'm about to *leave*. I'm about to get my dream. I have everyone I care about with me. I'm escaping the planet I hate.

For the first time, I'm about to fly through the stars.

And I'm on this gorgeous, beautiful, advanced machine.

I'm one of the lucky ones.

I'm going to escape.

And it's because of Valen.

I swallow around the lump in my throat when I think of his name.

I can't. I can't think about him right now.

We move up a few places, and my heart starts thrashing in my throat when we're up next. I reach over and grab my father's hand. He looks over at me with his gray eyes. "I'm sorry, Nova. I tried to keep you safe. I thought Korpillion was safe."

I shake my head. "You did keep me safe," I say, squeezing his hand. "You couldn't have known."

I think there's more he wants to say, but Zayne interrupts.

"Hold on to something," he says as he grabs the bar that hangs down from the roof of the ship. "Here we go!"

And I slide back against my seat, hard, as the ship picks up speed. I thought it would be bumpy and feel out of control, when I imagined what it must feel like to take off in one of these ships.

But it's smooth as steel. It's like an arrow being shot.

The brilliant lights of Korpillion become a blurred line. Immediately, they grow long and dim.

And there's this popping sound. Then it's dark.

For a brief second, I feel myself float in my seat, but the harnesses keep me from drifting off. It only lasts a second though, before the gravity simulators kick in, and I feel five hundred pounds in my seat.

# TWELVE

Within an hour, we're out of the solar system.

I can't even wrap my mind around it. I can't make it connect.

Just hours ago, I was running for my life on the same planet I grew up on. And now I'm not even in the same solar system. I can't see the same sun I've always known. I can't see the moon that has been the constant companion to Korpillion.

I'm out here, in space.

I am unanchored.

I'm free.

As soon as we got out of the system, the Frank again asked me where I wanted it to set as our destination.

"I need to think about it," I said.

I still have no idea.

So it put the ship into neutral, letting us glide through space on the same path we used to escape Korpillion. It's not a bad plan. We're still moving farther and farther away, and we're preserving our Neron core, saving energy.

The ship has everything we need. There are six bunks for sleeping in. There's a small restroom with everything we need. There's a tiny kitchen. The lounge is only a small round table behind the seats in the command deck, where the view opens up to the stars around us.

I don't think anyone is surprised when I find myself in the mechanical room. There are wires and pipes and tanks and motors. And there's the Neron core. It stands as tall as I am, and just about as round. It glows brilliant blue, swirling and pulsing with energy.

I place my hand on the glass that keeps it contained. It feels warm, but not hot.

I let my eyes slide closed.

I can feel it. I'm aware of every corner of it, its exact weight.

I'm not even touching it, but I feel incredible.

I feel connected and grounded and free and wild.

"I didn't know."

The words slip through the blockade I'd tried to put between our minds before I even give them permission to. But it's just natural. As easy as breathing. That tunnel, the connection, it's just there. Like a part of my brain.

"I believe you," his voice fills my head with such clarity.

The image of his face fills my mind. His smooth, flawless skin. His narrow lips. His deep brows, guarding his glowing eyes. Hair as black as the night. A presence that dominated the entire planet.

"Do you wish I had told you?" he asks when I'm quiet for a good, solid minute. "Who I am?"

I take my time finding my answer. I have to search, deep in my soul. I have to ask myself, *am I a good person?* "No," I answer honestly.

"I only regret that you had to see me…like the rest of the galaxy sees me." I hear that regret in his voice.

"Are you saying that's not the real you?" I ask, a hint of anger creeping into my voice. "The uniform? The mask? The power?"

I get this…impression from him. Of depth. Of falling. Of darkness. Of pain. Of loneliness.

"You know who I am, Nova."

The breath floats out of my chest as my lips fall open. Emotions spring into my eyes, and I clutch my hands to my chest.

Because I *can* feel him. I feel as if I just fell down into his own chest, right into the chambers of his heart.

I'm consumed by rage and confusion and dark. So much dark.

So much pain.

I feel so alone.

"Valen," I whisper, the name tasting complex and…*right* on my lips. "What happened to you?"

He doesn't respond, but he lets me sit there in his heart, gathering the true weight of…him. I feel it, I taste it, I breathe it.

Valen is not a good man. The level of compassion in him starves me, the anger and the bitterness in his blood could fuel *The Dominion* for centuries.

But he is an empty vessel. He wants to be filled. With something. With hope. With…a reason.

But he is a man who has never felt either of those things.

"Valen, I…" But I don't know what to say. I remember his touch, the feeling of having him right there, right in front of me. Of him touching me, even for just a brief moment.

I feel empty now that he is not here, right in front of me right now.

And I feel that same feeling reciprocated back at me.

"Did you see anything?" he asks. His voice begs for the truth. "When we touched. Did you see anything?"

Immediately, I see it in my mind. The destroyed planet behind us. Our dark clothing. The black crowns.

But mostly, I remember the love.

It was obvious on every inch of our faces.

"Yes," I whisper, my voice hoarse. "Did you?"

"I saw the future," he says. "I saw us, together. But we were different people. What I saw was an absolute impossibility."

His words hurt. I don't know what exactly it was that he saw. But his words hurt.

But they're true.

And they loosen my chest just a little.

*We were different people.*

*What I saw was an absolute impossibility.*

"That's what I saw," I say the words, even though I hate them.

I want him to take them back.

But I have to face the truth. I have to remember that the love I saw, that I felt, for just a moment, isn't real.

I have to remember who Valen is.

Tears slip from my eyes. Because another image of him returns to me. Of him standing in the Square. Of him forming that Neron spear. Of him shooting it through those miners, killing them.

I know Valen can feel me thinking about the scene, and another impression settles into me. He doesn't try to justify what he did. He accepts it. It is a part of him, the same as his Neron blue eyes.

"Why did you help me?" I finally ask as I wipe the tears away. "Why couldn't you have given me more warning? Why didn't you save others?"

"Because you aren't nothing, Nova," Valen says. "I know there is a reason we formed this bond, and I need you."

His last three words resound in my heart, over and over and over again.

*I need you.*

I don't want them to form in my head, but they do, the words, *I need you too.*

He doesn't answer my last two questions, and I feel it, he won't explain or justify anything.

Valen Nero does not give explanations. He does not apologize for his actions.

There's something broken inside of him. I feel it like it is as big as a mountain, somehow existing inside of his body.

"You need to go somewhere safe, Nova," Valen says, moving along. "Please don't tell me where you're going." I feel it: he means it. He doesn't want Cyrillius to ever use the Kinduri to make him tell Dominion where I am. But he did make that threat, that promise, *I will come for you, Nova.* "You need to find somewhere isolated. And you need to learn how to wield your abilities."

"Valen, I'm not-"

"It will be easier if you just accept it," he cuts me off. But his voice is calm. "Self-hatred and self-denial has never made anyone a better person. You are a Nero, Nova."

There. He said it. Like it is simple. Like it is a fact.

I can't be a Nero. Valen is the only Nero born in eighty-seven solars. I'm from Korpillion, a planet with only a little Neron.

I guess I don't know that.

Korpillion's entire core could be made of Neron.

Maybe it's not entirely impossible.

"I don't know what that means," I admit. "I don't know what that means for my future. I don't know if that means there's something I should be doing, right now. I don't know how to figure this out on my own."

I instantly feel incredibly lonely.

But there's that pressure in my mind, the presence.

*No.* Actually, I'm not alone.

The one person in the galaxy who would know how I'm feeling is already here in my head.

And there's that thought again: I need him. I need Valen, right here with me.

But I know what he's done. I know who he works for.

I need someone to guide me.

But I need, with everything in me, to not end up like him.

I know Valen can feel my thoughts. He doesn't respond with offence or anger. He agrees.

"I've heard that the Bahiri still exist," he says. His tone is quiet, like he doesn't think he should be telling me this information. "I've only heard rumors. But rumors are usually based in truth. You will be safest with them."

The Bahiri? How could they still exist when the only known

Nero is Valen, the very opposite of what they believe in? They exist because they have hope in the Nero, that they can make the galaxy a better place again. They worship the Nero and Neron.

They still exist?

"Do you know where they are?" I ask.

"No," he states simply. "Find them, stay safe. Stay good, Nova."

I feel him start to close the connection, but I throw out a frantic thought, like throwing out a hand to stop a door from closing.

"You don't have to be like this, Valen," I say, desperate. "You don't have to stay with Dominion. You're so much stronger than Cyrillius. Your life could be so much better doing good things."

The feeling of Valen is heavy. Weighted. Depressed. "I thought there was no more good, Nova. I thought we were all out for gain."

I remember the conversation we had, not long ago. I was doubtful then, too.

I shake my head, even though he can't see it.

"It might be hard to find," I say. "But there is good. Walk away from him, Valen. Don't be his puppet."

I know I've said the wrong thing, because I feel him harden. I feel bristles and spikes rise.

"Get far away from Korpillion, Nova," he says. "Find the Bahiri, and never look back."

And just like that, I feel him close the door between our minds.

# THIRTEEN

Zayne and I sit in the seats, looking out the viewport. The Frank sits in its seat, but at the moment, it's powered down. I still haven't given him a direction to head.

It's so dark out here. Little specks of light dot the view before us, but they're few and far between.

Reena walks in, sitting in the seat next to Zayne.

"So are we still just aimlessly floating out here, wasting our supplies?" she asks.

She knows she can't say too much, because she's just lucky we haven't kicked her out into space to freeze and die. But she is being logical.

"Reena, have you heard any rumors that there are still any Bahiri left?" I ask. I look back at her, but try not to seem too interested. I haven't told anyone on board yet what happened just before we left

Korpillion. I still don't believe it, myself.

"The Bahiri?" she asks. "Thought they were all just legends. I can't imagine any of them are still around. There aren't any Nero around for them to worship. Valen Nero certainly isn't what they once revered."

Footsteps pull my eyes back to the door that leads into the living quarters. Dad walks in, coming to sit in the seat behind Zayne. "I know there are a few of them left. Heard they had all retreated back to the E sector," he says as he settles into his seat.

The E sector? That's forever away. It would take us a solar to get there, and that's if we didn't stop for supplies, which we're going to have to do soon.

"What planets are even in the E sector?" Zayne asks. "Can't say I know a single thing about that side of the galaxy."

Dad shakes his head. "Can't say that I really know. It's just what I heard."

"I've heard that all the planets in the F and G sector don't have Neron," Reena says. "Supposedly, Dominion doesn't have a single planet out that way."

And it sparks a light. If the Bahiri are in E, we could head toward F or G and ask questions along the way.

"I say we go there, then," I say, speaking up. "After what we saw happen on Korpillion, I want nothing to do with Dominion. I'll be glad to be as far away from their reach as possible."

"It would take us nine lunars just to reach the G sector," Zayne points out. "It's forever away."

"If it means peace, wouldn't the time be worth it?" Torin says. He looks up at Zayne with heavy eyes before they slide to me. And I know, if it means peace and keeping us safe, he'll travel wherever, no matter how long it takes.

"We'll have to make quite a few supply stops," Reena says. I'm surprised she's on board. After a life of crime, I would think she wouldn't run and hide so quickly, but maybe her lifestyle has taken its toll.

I nod. "We have enough to last us another six days. Frank." His eyes light up and his head turns in my direction. "How far is the nearest planet with supplies?"

He pauses for a moment. "The nearest inhabited planet is Stippe. We would land in five days' time."

"Is Dominion on that planet?" Zayne asks.

Another pause from the Frank. "No, Dominion's presence is not found on Stippe."

I look around at my little family. We're bound together now, brought into one another's lives permanently by fleeing a doomed planet. But we're here now.

They may not know why I want to reach the E sector, but after three days of aimlessly floating through space, I know they're just happy to have a plan.

I'm going to take Valen's advice.

I'm going to find the Bahiri.

And get some answers.

"Frank," I say. "Our overall destination is the G sector. But take us to Stippe for supplies."

"Yes, Nova," he answers flatly. His fingers plug into the controls.

And every one of us barely get two seconds to buckle up before the Neron core surges, and we rocket forward through space, bound for a planet far from here.

# THE END OF
# EPISODE ONE

# ABOUT THE AUTHOR

Keary Taylor is the *USA Today* bestselling author of over twenty novels. She grew up along the foothills of the Rocky Mountains where she started creating imaginary worlds and daring characters who always fell in love. She now splits her time between a tiny island in the Pacific Northwest and Utah, dragging along her husband and their two children. She continues to have an overactive imagination that frequently keeps her up at night.

To learn more about Keary and her books, please visit
WWW.KEARYTAYLOR.COM

Made in the USA
Middletown, DE
20 January 2019